REINS OF FRIENDSHIP
HEIDI HERMAN

LIFE'S A RODEO • PREQUEL

REINS OF FRIENDSHIP

A NOVELLA

HEIDI HERMAN

PINK VIKING
PRESS

All rights reserved. No part of this book may be reproduced or transmitted in any form or by any means, electronic or mechanical, including photocopying, recording, or by any information storage and retrieval system, without the written permission of the author, except where permitted by law.

This is a work of fiction. All characters, organizations, and events portrayed in this novella are products of the author's imagination and are used fictitiously.

This book was written and edited by a human author, and the cover was designed by a human, without the use of generative AI. This publication or its contents cannot be used to train generative AI technologies or to generate text without the author's exclusive rights under copyright.

Cover design by KAM.design
Edited by Vanessa Lebans
Formatting by F + P Graphic Design

Pink Viking Press, a division of Hekla Publishing LLC
1603 Capitol Ave
Suite 310-A431
Cheyenne, Wyoming 82001
www.HeklaPublishing.com

Copyright © 2025 Heidi Herman
All rights reserved.

ISBN Paperback: 978-1-947233-15-7
ISBN eBook: need — optional
Library of Congress Control Number: 2025920387
First edition | Printed in USA

*Friendship isn't about
who you've known the longest;
it's about who walked into your life
and said, 'I'm here for you'
and proved it.*
—Cowboy Quotes

CONTENTS

1 Arrival...9

2 Dinner on the Deck........................19

3 Morning Coffee..............................27

4 Shopping & a Rescue Cat.................35

5 Dinner in the Village......................47

6 Saturday Night Firepit Chat.............57

7 Sunday Morning Brunch..................63

8 Departure 73

Author's Note...................................79

About the Author..............................89

1
ARRIVAL

"Double-check those directions again, Jo, could you? We've gone more than three miles." Moirin Garrett squinted as she searched for another tiny green sign. The city planners had done a terrific job of camouflaging street signs to the point where they were nearly useless. She was all for blending civilization with the environment, but this was ridiculous.

"Um, I think this is right. Right, right, left." Jo mumbled, rocking her head from side to side as she studied the map on her phone. "Yeah, no, this is it. Should just be a couple more minutes." Her friend shrugged and dropped the phone onto her lap.

"If you're sure," Moirin said. "At least it's been a beautiful drive. It is so nice to be taking a vacation."

"Taking a half-day off on a Friday is not a vacation," Jo scoffed. "You've always been a little too committed to your family's business, but ever since you and Ellis broke up, I have to tell you, girlfriend, I'm worried you'll become a workaholic."

Moirin scoffed. "Workaholic is a bit much. I'm just very focused right now. But Ellis would probably agree with you. He said I always put the company before our relationship, and that's why he ended things." At home alone in the empty condo, those accusations played on a loop in her mind, so staying later at the office each day meant more tasks to occupy her time and fewer hours wondering if she made the right choice.

Although truthfully, he hadn't given her much of a choice. Just a *sorry, hon, this isn't working out,* then severed all contact. At least they hadn't lived together, so there was no awkward packing or moving out. Just goodbye.

"Oh, slow down. That's our turn." Jo pointed to what looked like an opening in the overgrown brush. "I never thought you guys had a future. I told you that more than once." She shook her head. "Neither of you was committed to anything. You didn't have any interests in common. Your entire relationship consisted of dinner together a couple of nights a week and being each other's plus-one at events. He wasn't husband material."

Moirin maneuvered the Audi between low-hanging branches, hoping to avoid scratches to the paint job. "Apparently, he is for someone. I saw his engagement photo in the paper this morning."

"You're kidding," Jo nearly gasped at the news. "Are you okay? You actually seem okay."

Moirin shrugged. Admitting it out loud wasn't as painful as she feared. It didn't generate a pang of regret or anything close to jealousy. She didn't feel cold-hearted, but honestly content in his newfound happiness. "I think I am. Maybe you were right. I hadn't been emotionally invested in him, and pursuing a deeper relationship would have been a mistake." With a landmark birthday looming, it was getting a little late in life to be thinking about marriage anyway. Maybe that ship had sailed. If not, she hoped he'd recognize the spark of romance when it finally came. And that she would be open to adding a special someone to her life

"1437. That driveway on your left." Jo waved, leaning in front of her. Moirin pushed her head back against the headrest, attempting to avoid Jo's flailing hand.

She pulled into the driveway and parked next to a sparkling black Pacifica. "Well, it looks like Heather managed to get Leslie out of the house on time. I was a little worried we'd arrive only to be sitting here waiting for them, with no way of getting into the house."

Jo chuckled. "Knowing Heather, she showed up to Leslie's place a couple of hours early and packed for her."

"She does have that big sister control gene, doesn't she?" Moirin stepped out of the car, stretched, and took a deep breath of the pine-scented air. They were only a few hours from Denver, but the lake sat three thousand feet higher, and the crisp, fresh air seemed like a thousand miles from the skyscrapers and traffic and a million miles from her non-stop corporate executive career. "I am so glad Heather arranged this weekend. We all needed it."

"Ooh, that's an understatement. I'd like to social distance myself from the past couple of years, you know? Wow, this place is gorgeous, isn't it?" Jo stood by the passenger side of the car, staring up at the stone and timber structure, which was immense yet masterfully built to blend perfectly with the surrounding forest. Brown, rust, and beige-colored stones, separated by massive wooden beams, gave the house a rustic feel that could easily be mistaken for a lodge, given its sheer size.

Moirin nodded, soaking in the surroundings. Birdsong trilled from hidden perches in branches high above them, as the breeze shook a staccato accompaniment from the leaves like a brush on a steel drum. Insects chirping and croaking added a rhythmic contribution, and the gentle sounds of water blended like a relaxing jazz score. They had driven past a house less than a half a mile away, but the spruce, fir, and pine trees grew so thick that she felt a sense of utter privacy.

She lingered, drinking in the scenery as she retrieved their bags from the trunk. Heather had done well, arranging their first post-pandemic girls' getaway, judging by the exterior of the house. The timing was perfect, using the end of summer weekend to celebrate her fiftieth birthday just weeks before Heather's fifty-second birthday.

"But, like I said, everything works out in the end. Fifty is proving to be a great year for me, and it might be a turning point for you, too." Moirin became aware that her best friend was still chattering.

Jo could talk non-stop, jumping from one topic to another without taking a breath sometimes. She had proven that during the drive when she updated Moirin on everything from her new job to the sale of a commercial building she's held on to for years, and her continuing efforts to appease her step-siblings' constant demands on behalf of their aging parents, despite the fact they talked at least once a week and Moirin was already cognizant of each topic. It was easy to tune most of it out, offering an occasional 'uh-huh' while she contemplated her recommendations for the seats becoming vacant on the company's Board of Directors and a plethora of other topics that demanded her attention as an executive officer of an international energy company.

"Well, here's to hoping that's true." Moirin hefted her overnight bag over one shoulder and picked up Jo's from the trunk. "I've got the luggage if you can grab those groceries out of the back."

"Deal." Jo grabbed the three canvas bags filled with provisions and trailed after Moirin up the flagstone path to the front door. Copper light fixtures and accents gave an elegant look to the covered patio, where cushioned rocking chairs sat, inviting guests to take a relaxing break from a long day.

They entered the house, and their every movement sent echoes reverberating through the twenty-foot wood beam ceiling. Standing in the foyer, Moirin looked around. An open door on her left revealed a small study filled with books. She guessed the two closed doors on the right were likely a closet and a lavatory. A short corridor on the left led to the kitchen. In front and to the right was an open combination dining room and family room.

Moirin left their bags in the foyer and stepped into the living room. It was tastefully decorated with natural tones of brown and linen, with subtle accents of green. Two seating areas with soft-looking leather couches were arranged, one around a large fireplace, and the other facing an expanse of windows. The gleaming wood floors were covered by several large area rugs with blue, green, and brown forest designs.

Someone must have spent hours scouring stores for the accents of bears, elk, and birds that seemed to be everywhere.

A full glass wall brought the outdoors inside, the blue, sparkling lake seeming only a few steps away. French doors flanked the fireplace, opening to a wrap-around deck.

"Oh, they're outside," Jo said. "Why don't you join them, and I'll be out once I put the groceries away?

Moirin glanced at Jo, shifting her weight as she hefted the bags. "Are you sure you don't need help?"

"Pshwah, I've got this." She hummed as she disappeared toward the kitchen.

Moirin headed out to the deck, drawn by the picturesque scene. It was even more stunning when she stepped outside.

"Hey, birthday girl." Leslie cried, jumping up to greet her. "Glad you made it. This place is amazing, isn't it?"

"It's beautiful," Moirin said. She hugged Leslie, then stepped over to Heather, who had been lounging on one of several wicker loveseats. She leaned down to give Heather a brief hug and air-kiss near her cheek. "Thank you, and happy early birthday to you."

She sat in the chair next to Heather and looked across the deck. There was seating for easily a dozen people, with an outdoor kitchen, complete with a bar and a half dozen barstools.

"It's something, isn't it?" Heather said. "It belongs to a surgeon Tabor works with. I guess they haven't used it in a few years, but they still have someone come in every week to clean and have it ready." She shook her head, as if marveling at the waste.

Moirin never understood her frugality. Heather was a physical therapist, and her husband, Tabor, was a vascular surgeon. They only had one child, but Heather budgeted as if they had a dozen children in a one-income household. Moirin understood she'd had a tough childhood, but she thought it was far past time for Heather to start enjoying her life's success.

Moirin was single but still had a housekeeper come twice a week. Her parents had live-in help to manage their five-thousand-square-foot house, which had always seemed more necessary than extravagant, given the number of parties and social gatherings they hosted. Their professions and standing in the community almost demanded it.

Leslie squealed again as Jo walked outside, carrying a tray crowded with appetizers, glasses, and a glass pitcher of lemonade. As Leslie took the tray and set it on the table, Heather got up and tugged on her wrinkled capris to straighten them.

"So good to see you, honey," Heather said, wrapping Jo in a bear hug.

"Hey, girl, you look fabulous. Is that scarf new? I love that color on you." Leslie playfully pushed her sister out of the way to step beside Jo, giving her a brief side-hug before spinning around to the table where she'd placed the appetizers.

Grabbing a handful, Leslie plopped down on a chair across from Moirin. "How was the drive?"

"Great. I got out of the office by noon, and we made good time here. Just stopped in the village for supplies. When did you guys get here?"

"Oh, like three hours ago. You know Heather. She insisted we get an early start in case we needed to clean here or something." She flipped her long hair, then combed it through her fingers and began braiding.

Leslie was only two years younger than Moirin and Jo but looked closer to five. Moirin was always a bit envious of her tawny-colored hair that would hide the inevitable gray far more than her own auburn or Jo's brunette hair. As Heather sat down beside her, Moirin noted the loose-flowing blouse and guessed it hid a few more pounds added since the last time they'd been together. They had only talked on the phone for the last few months, but she'd complained about weight gain. She looked worn and tired. Moirin hoped it was just an adjustment and that Heather didn't have a greater struggle going on that she was keeping to herself.

Leslie leaned over and chatted with Jo, their laughter floating on the breeze to Moirin. She had tuned out their conversation but smiled, hoping they'd think she was listening. Heather poured a glass of lemonade and loaded up a napkin with cheese and crackers Jo had prepared. She looked at Moirin, raising her eyebrow and nodding toward the lemonade.

Moirin shook her head, "No thanks. I'm just going to sit back and enjoy a sun soak."

She watched as Heather settled back in the chair, joining the conversation with Jo and Leslie. Since she'd met them in college, the two sisters had always been different, but the years seemed to exaggerate their differences. Leslie's free-flowing bohemian style matched her artistic nature. Over the years, her face had become thinner, the glasses she'd started wearing made her look frailer somehow, but her brown eyes were still empathetic and kind. Heather's face was a bit rounder than in their college years, but her long pageboy hairstyle was the same. Her trendy wardrobe had been replaced by casual clothes and comfortable shoes, like the blue-and-white Keds she was wearing. A fringe cloche was pulled down onto her forehead, shading her eyes. She looked comfortable and settled into her life.

Moirin often felt like she was still on the fast track to success, waiting for the comfortable and settled days. *Am I missing out on the good years?* No, of course not. Fifty was hardly old. It was all this birthday nonsense and the shock of seeing an ex's engagement announcement that had her so pensive. She needed to snap out of it. She shifted her thoughts with a mental shake. *Focus on fun, or help Heather embrace her empty nest years.* Something besides work and her single status.

A few hours later, the snacks had disappeared, and the drink pitcher sat empty. The sun had ducked behind the tree line. It was hours yet before sunset, but the breeze was stronger, and a slight chill had settled in the air.

"Why don't we do a quick tour, and all get settled in our rooms?" Heather stood up and brushed her hands together.

"That sounds good. I'm all sweaty from sitting out here. I'd love a shower before dinner," Jo said.

"I should check my email. Keeping up on things will make for a better Monday next week," Moirin said.

"Ah-hah." Leslie snickered as she stood and threw an arm around Jo's shoulder. In a loud stage-whisper, she said, "We really need to stage an intervention for that one before workaholicism sets in completely."

"Very funny. You and Jo are in cahoots, huh? Only an hour, then, and I'll come back downstairs to help with dinner. I promise."

"Oh, girls, leave her alone," Heather said. "Grab your bags and follow me upstairs. Leslie and I chose rooms already, and there are two more for you guys."

"You guys go ahead, I already settled in, so I'm going to go down and take a walk by the lake," Leslie said.

Moirin followed Heather upstairs, Jo trailing after her. She was pleased to see that each bedroom had a queen-size bed, cozy-looking club chairs, and a writing desk. Even better, each had a private attached bath. It was hard to believe this was a vacation home; someone had furnished it like a high-end bed-and-breakfast.

Jo disappeared into the first available room, and Moirin walked into a similar one across the hall.

"Okay, I'll leave you to get settled in. I'm going to call and check on Camilla." Heather tapped the doorframe. Moirin nodded, admiring the lake view before unpacking her bag and hanging her clothes in the closet.

She settled at the desk and set up her laptop, opening her work email once the machine powered up. As always, there were a few dozen new messages. She scanned the list, and one with the subject line "Board Candidates" from her father caught her attention, and she clicked to open it.

I've reviewed your candidate selections for the Board and understand the appeal of those who support green initiatives and climate-friendly approaches to energy, if their CVs reflect successful financial management.

Ian has offered two names, as well. I'm ambivalent to the first but would turn down the second. I've heard enough about Gregorian Plankett that I'm convinced he would not be a good fit for us. Perhaps it would be best to pursue one of your selections and one of Ian's.

Moirin pursed her lips, contemplating a reply. Her father had served as Chairman of the Board for nearly a decade, while his younger brother, Ian, had the role of CEO. Moirin was the Chief Operations Officer but would be replacing Ian in a few years. The terms of two of his longtime associates were up, and another was retiring from the Board, so now was the time to restructure and seat members attuned to her vision.

She tapped the pen on her lip, weighing alternatives and considering her approach. She was not CEO yet, but the makeup of the Board was crucial to her future plans. Plans that needed to start now, while she was still COO. A plan was forming, but it needed time to fully develop.

Notepad next to the computer, she took notes while reviewing several other crucial messages, flipping back and forth as Board thoughts came to her. The successful future of the company depended on her making the right decisions in the next week, but the daily work didn't stop. Shadows grew in the world outside the window, but Moirin barely noticed. She snapped on the lamp when the room started to become dim, her eyes never looking up from the computer screen.

2
DINNER ON THE DECK

Jo hummed as she moved through the kitchen, happy that life was finally under control, and the constant sense of impending doom had faded. It wasn't just the pandemic ending, which was great, but the darkness of the past seven years was lifting. Snippets of Disney tunes and feel-good sixties songs mixed with a few church choruses in her mind as she be-bopped around the spacious kitchen.

"I'm so happy, hap-hap-happy, chim-chim-cheree. If you're happy and you know it, say amen. A-men." She broke into song, spinning as she tried a choreographed-like move to open the refrigerator, nearly crashing into the door instead. She heard a chuckle behind her.

She turned to see Leslie settle herself on one of the barstools at the island, plopping her head down to rest her chin in her hands. "I came in to see if you wanted help." Jo saw the grin pulling at her mouth.

"What? It's okay, you can laugh at my kitchen-dancing. It was much smoother in my head." She sniffed, opening the refrigerator, and pulling out a white paper-wrapped package.

Leslie eyed it suspiciously. "So, did you see the article I sent you about the benefits of a vegetarian diet?"

"Um, no, I don't think I read that one yet." Jo held the package up. "We stopped at the market, and I picked up this smoked lake trout. I thought we could have it with Mediterranean basmati rice and green salad. I also got a fresh sourdough from the bakery and a very mild lemon horseradish butter you're gonna love to go with it."

"Mmm, that sounds delicious." Leslie cocked her head. "And fish is so healthy, right? They say you should really avoid red meat. And sourdough has all those prebiotics, right? I read you should try to get more fiber and fermented foods for healthy gut microbiomes."

"Yup, it's all pretty good for you." Jo stooped to search the lower cabinet for a baking tray, hoping to hide her grin. Leslie must have read the new copy of *Women's Health* cover to cover and probably memorized half of it. She located a tray and put it on the island countertop, then turned and set the oven to preheat.

"So, Heather said everything is done now with your building sale," Leslie said.

Jo unwrapped the fish, smoothing the paper out on the counter, staring at it for a moment. Even now, her heart clenched a little thinking about that building. Selling it had been bittersweet. It had been the cornerstone of her husband's entrepreneurial dreams, but the business died with him seven years before. She had hung on to the building for the rental income, but the tenant's business didn't survive the pandemic.

She pushed the melancholy aside, forcing a smile for Leslie. "Yes, I closed on it a couple of weeks ago. I felt guilty, you know, it being the last connection to Erik's dreams and all, but it was time. The lump sum of cash in the bank means a whole lot more to me than a little rental income and the constant upkeep and taxes. Still, I was sad to see it go."

Leslie clucked her tongue and frowned. "Aw, honey, that's okay. He *would have understood. I'm surprised you never opened a restaurant in that space yourself. With the way you cook, you would have done great.*"

"That's sweet, but I don't think I could ever have a restaurant. I'd be afraid it would take all the fun out of cooking for me." She stood on her tiptoes, grunting as she grasped at the shelf, her fingertips only brushing the edge. "Ugh. Okay, stretch, would you get that salad bowl down and wipe it out for me?"

"Sure, munchkin." Leslie walked over, reached over Jo's head, and pulled down the bowl as Jo tossed a kitchen towel on the island.

"I never liked owning commercial property, you know? So much responsibility." Jo laid smoked trout in rows on the tray. "Just having the house is enough for me. It's mine and no one can take it away."

"You're so lucky that your mortgage is paid off. You and Erik did a good job of life planning. Most people in their forties don't think about life insurance, especially when they don't have kids."

Jo stopped, a familiar tiny knife twinge of pain rippling through her heart that seemed to freeze her in a moment of loss.

Leslie clapped her hand over her mouth and cringed. "Oh, honey, I'm sorry, that was thoughtless."

Over the years, it faded in frequency and intensity, but moments like this reminded Jo it would never go away. She always wanted to be a mother, but it seemed it wasn't to be; then suddenly, she was a widow. She doubted she could have crawled her way out of depression after his death without her friends. But she was stronger now. At this point, she could probably handle anything life threw at her.

"It's okay. Sometimes it just takes me by surprise." Jo patted Leslie's hand. She shifted the conversation, preferring to focus on positive thoughts. "And now that I'm back into marketing full-time, I'm having fun working again. It's challenging, and I'm making decent money. That was the only good thing about Covid - all the time at home so I could take online classes." She slid the trout into the oven.

Leslie says, "Who knows? Maybe someday you'll go into business for yourself doing marketing."

"Oh, no way. It's great finally getting a regular paycheck. Being self-employed is hard, and too much responsibility. It's more fun, too, just being part of the team and not the boss. Most everybody else is younger but I'm like a den mother or something. I bring in muffins and they come to me for advice. All in all, I'm really happy where I'm at."

Leslie swished the towel around in the bowl. "Yeah, I get that. I feel that way about going back to the classroom. Trying to teach remotely was so depressing. All those tiny screens staring back at me were eating away at my soul. I can't wait to see all those happy little faces with their giggles and silly questions." She sighed, clutching the damp dish towel to her chest.

"Hey, I'm glad you're doing so much better." Jo extended her open hand across the counter, and Leslie grabbed it, squeezing. "I know we both went through some dark times the past few years, but it's bright times ahead, right? A positive attitude goes a long way."

"Yes. I take it one day at a time and have faith that one of these days I'll have my boys back. That, and your Miss Pollyanna sunshine, is all the support I need. You could find the silver lining in a derecho cloud."

Jo laughed. "Okay, well, this fish will be ready in a few minutes, so I'll make the rice and toss the salad if you'll set up the table outside? It's such a perfect evening."

"You got it." Leslie shuffled back and forth with plates, silverware, and glasses, then helped Jo take the serving dishes outside. Leslie went to round up Moirin and Heather while Jo mixed a pitcher of iced tea.

Once they gathered at the table, Moirin raised her iced tea in a toast.

"To us. We've aged, but we're all still those same girls who met at CU Boulder. We've stuck together through some crazy times over the years." She directed her glass at each one of them in turn. "Thank you for being here. I love you guys. Cheers."

"Cheers," They each echoed, raising their glasses and clinking.

"Okay, Moirin, I love you too, but pass that platter of trout. I want to dig in before it gets cold."

"Jo, this smells amazing," Heather said. "Thank you for cooking." She slid a filet of trout from the platter to her plate, then passed it on.

The bowls of salad and rice followed the platter until their plates were full. For several minutes, the only sound was that of flatware scraping against stoneware plates.

"This trout is heavenly, and that horseradish butter is so good. Thank you for all of this."

"My pleasure. The kitchen setup they have here is fantastic. What I wouldn't give for a kitchen like that in my house."

"This whole house is fantastic. And the property is gorgeous. I mean, look at this view," Leslie said, spreading her arm toward the lake. "How could someone own something so beautifully perfect and not use it?"

"If I had a place like this, I would love to host barbeques and family get-togethers," Jo said.

"I don't understand it," Heather said. "It seems like a waste. I mean, really, what do they do out here that's different from home?"

"Oh, I totally get it," Leslie said, looking toward the lake. "Martin and I used to take the boys camping, and we'd go hiking and fishing. Every night, we'd sit around a fire toasting marshmallows and making s'mores. Then we'd tell stories and laugh and laugh. The boys just loved it. I miss their laughter."

"Well, I'm happy we're all here together this weekend." Jo forced a broad smile and squeezed Leslie's hand. "The rest of life will still be there on Monday, but right now, it's girls' time to make some memories, right?"

"Absolutely," Moirin said. "You know, when we first arrived, one of my first thoughts was how nice it would be to have a place like this one day." Moirin folded her hands, then looked out over the lake.

"Not anymore?" Jo rarely saw her friend in such a pensive mood.

"No, you guys were right a minute ago. This is a house for families. I think Uncle Ian or even Colin should have a house like this, not me."

"Oh, Moirin. Don't say that." Leslie looked stricken.

Moirin shook her head. "No, it's all right. I've been thinking about Ellis. Jo was right. I don't miss him as much as I should. Maybe that's because he wasn't the right one for me, or maybe I just have other priorities in my life. It would be nice if it were a bit of both. This opportunity I have to restructure the board could change everything. My dad and uncle Ian have made the company very successful and, of course, I want to continue that success, but in my own way. To achieve my goals, I need the board to think as I do, so I need to get like-minded people in place now.

"That's smart," Heather said, leaning forward. "I can tell you from current experience that being constantly at odds with a management team is exhausting and time-consuming. The couple who owns the clinic I run are never in agreement. One agrees with me, and the other fights an idea. The crazy thing is, I never know which will agree and which will dissent on any issue. Get people on the Board who support the direction you're moving." She raised her glass, winking at Moirin before taking a long drink.

Moirin smiled. "Thank you for that. Environmentally responsible energy and corporate profits needn't be mutually exclusive. And I think focusing on creating a legacy like that, rather than romantic relationships, for now, is an acceptable trade-off. I don't regret ending things with Ellis, but I think I *would* regret not putting my full focus into changing the company's path. I don't intend to be a reclusive workaholic." She looked around the table. "I'll find balance, you'll see. And you three will always be important to me. Other people, too, at some point."

Heather chuckled.

"So, let's plan on making memories, then," Jo said.

"I'd love to check out more of the village. We just stopped to pick up some food but didn't explore. Did you guys see anything yet?" Jo looked from Leslie to Heather.

"No, we drove straight here," Heather said. "It looked quaint, though. It would be fun to go there tomorrow."

"I want to jog some of the trails by the lake in the morning, but the village sounds fun." Moirin nodded.

"I'm game," Leslie said. "But right now, would you pass me some more of that salad, please?"

The rest of the food disappeared as they gossiped, talked, and laughed. Most of all, they laughed. When the evening wound down, Heather insisted on cleaning up. "It's the least I can do after such a nice dinner. You guys go ahead. I've got this."

Jo hugged her. "Thanks, mom." She laughed as Heather swatted at her but missed. Jo chuckled as she followed Moirin and Leslie upstairs.

3
MORNING COFFEE

Leslie relished the early morning chill. On most days, she used the living room in her apartment, but sometimes she had time to join the sunrise group at the park. Being by herself, completely immersed in nature, was a decadent luxury. The yoga mat was soft and springy, padding her feet from the hard wooden planks of the deck. Even without the mat, it was the perfect spot for morning meditation. The lake sparkled in random spots as tiny beams of morning sunshine found their way through the trees. Birds trilled and chirped, singing from the trees, and several landed on the railing next to her. There was something elemental and peaceful about wildlife blissfully ignoring her and going about their daily business.

Closing her eyes, she reached up, feeling the pull from her fingertips up her arm. As she bent, the satisfying stretch lengthened across her ribs and into her hip. She inhaled, savoring the spicy, pine-scented air of the forest. Today, she completed an entire hour-long routine with more detailed flows and longer holds than normal. No clock-watching today, worried about arriving at work on time, or rushing to a photography gig. She felt utterly at peace even before meditation.

She wondered how long she would have this pristine world to herself before the others were up and around. Even though Heather and Jo slept late, Moirin was already up, out on a morning run. She had waved when she cut across the deck to the path along the water. It had been an hour, so she should be back soon. Leslie took a deep breath and exhaled, counting to ten. *Hurried stress isn't the path to peaceful meditation.*

She settled on the mat, sitting cross-legged with her hands placed palm-up, one on top of the other. Closing her eyes, she let the sounds and scents of the forest consume her focus, clearing her mind of cluttering thoughts. Her heart rate slowed, and her shoulders dropped, every muscle giving in to relaxation. Reaching for her phone, she skimmed over the apps and opened one of several she had loaded. The chimes refocused her thoughts for the next ten minutes, then, checking to ensure she was still alone, she switched to her daily pledge and milestone app, a part of her ongoing recovery. She was committed to sobriety, but it was easier when it was private.

Feeling refreshed and invigorated, Leslie stood and rolled up her mat, sticking it under her arm. She walked to the edge of the deck, leaning on the railing, looking out over the forest and lake. Her fingers itched for her camera, as her eyes framed shots of landscape, birds, and a fuzzy-tailed squirrel that chattered incessantly at her.

A flash of blue from the trail drew her attention. Moirin was headed back. Leslie promised herself she would take the same trail later and capture awe-inspiring and gorgeous shots. She waved before turning and going inside.

Heather and Jo sat in the dining room, sipping coffee, a plate of muffins on the table between them.

"Good morning, sunshine," Jo said. "You're all vibrant and glowy this morning."

"Thanks. I'll take the vibrant, but I think the glowy is more like sweaty. I'm going to shower. I'll be back down in a bit."

"I'll save you a muffin," Heather said.

Leslie chuckled. Those muffins were going to be difficult to resist. Jo was an excellent cook, and her breakfast treats were better than any bakery Leslie had tried. Jo often brought cookies, sweet bread, or pies along whenever she visited anyone. Leslie often shared them with someone else. She'd gain two dress sizes if she ate them all.

Jo had been petite as long as Leslie had known her, but she ate more than any of them, indulging in her homemade treats as much as she shared. If she had a secret routine for supercharging her metabolism, it would be nice if she'd share that.

They should both probably eat healthier, but neither had ever learned to cook. Without a mother around to teach them those things, they couldn't be expected to know any better. It's too bad the one thing she had inherited was her mother's addictive personality.

Nope, not going there. She shook her head as she ran up the stairs two at a time. There's no sense in finding peace if you're going to let your mind go back to old wounds. Daisy's words echoed as loudly as if her sponsor had been standing beside her.

It's a beautiful day, in a beautiful place, surrounded by good friends. It's going to be a good day. She repeated the mantra as she showered and dressed in a pale green chiffon and ruffle mini dress. She braided her hair and applied a light layer of tinted sunscreen and mascara. Feeling pretty, she bounded downstairs, eager for her first cup of coffee.

She rummaged in the refrigerator, pulling out the packaged yogurt and granola she'd brought. Filling a mug with coffee, she joined Heather and Jo at the table, their heads close together, deep in conversation.

"It's just going to be so strange with Camilla gone," Heather said. "I should feel lucky she lived at home and took half her classes remotely last year. With Tabor's contacts, she's lined up a part-time job for clinical experience, so it makes sense for her to live in the dorms."

"The start of a new school year," Jo leaned back and looked at Leslie, shrugging as she took a sip of coffee.

"Oh, yeah. It's always bittersweet. I remember when the boys started school. In kindergarten, they were more upset than I was, but every year after that, I was blubbering, and they were fine." Leslie chuckled.

"I loved taking Camilla school shopping. We'd make a whole girl's day of it and buy clothes and shoes and all her supplies." Heather said. "Of course, then she became a teenager and was too cool for that. After that, she just wanted a few hundred dollars and would go to the mall with her friends."

"At least you had a girl," Leslie said. "The boys hated shopping."

Heather and Jo exchanged a look. Heather cocked her head as Jo took another sip of coffee.

"Hey, guys, it's okay. I like talking about them. I know I don't get time with them now, but that's why the memories are important, and I'm working on fixing things." Leslie peeled the cover from the yogurt and mixed in the crunchy granola.

"You know," Heather said. "If there's one thing I've learned, it's that life has its ups and downs. Think of where you were two years ago, compared to where you are today. Then think of two years from now, how different things will be."

"I know. Maybe I can have a showing of my photography or start writing poetry. Oh, maybe get a scuba certification." She twirled her spoon in the yogurt.

Jo laughed. "We live in Colorado. What are you going to do with a scuba certification?"

Footsteps sounded on the stairs, and Moirin rounded the corner into the kitchen. "Anyone need more coffee?"

"Yes, please," Jo shouted. "Just bring the pot."

"I don't know. I was watching a reality show where they were scuba diving, and it looked cool." Lesie shrugged.

Moirin joined them, setting the coffeepot next to the muffins. "Oh, blueberry. These look good. Thanks, Jo."

"I think you have a better shot with the photography," Heather said, reaching across the table to grab a muffin. She looked over at Leslie and grinned. "No pun intended."

Jo laughed.

Moirin nodded. "She's right. Your pictures are good. You should show them to a gallery and see what happens," she said between bites of muffin.

"I still think a scuba certification would be more fun," Leslie said. "But I'll give the gallery thing some thought. Hey, speaking of photos, let's finish breakfast and take our traditional girls getaway pic."

A chorus of groans echoed against the high ceilings.

"Oh, stop. We're making memories. And we need the photos so when we're old ladies and our memories are shot, we'll have nice pictures to remind us of all the good times."

"I suppose then I need to shower and change. I don't want any permanent evidence of this pajama party," Heather said. She dabbed at her mouth with a napkin, then stood, collecting her plate and coffee cup. Leslie heard the clatter of dishes in the sink, then the slow thumps of footsteps up the stairs.

"Ok, you guys finish here, and I'll set up the tripod. I check the lighting and see where the best background is." She walked away mumbling to herself about light, shine, and squinting.

An hour later, she lounged outside, reading a novel on her electronic reader. Moirin stepped out from the French door and took a deep breath. "I just want to spend all day outside here. It's so nice to be away from the office."

Leslie looked up. "Totally."

"As I say that, I came out here to get you. I think everyone's ready."

"Perfect," Leslie said. She checked the tripod in the living room, adjusting it slightly to account for the sun's movement. They tested the light meter a few more times and peered through the camera lens to test the background.

"Can you guys stand there so I can check the balance? Just don't stand too close together, so you'll cover more area like the four of us."

Jo and Moirin obediently moved into position. Moirin looked like a polished executive in her white linen ankle-length pants and green and white blouse with crisp cuffs at the elbow, her auburn hair slicked back and caught in a small ponytail. Jo wore a sleeveless white sundress accessorized with shimmering silver jewelry. Leslie nodded. Her own pale green minidress would complement their clothing colors.

Heather walked in, hugging her cell phone to her ear. "Yes, honey, of course. Just go to the bookstore and use your emergency credit card. What? Camilla Jean Santos!" Heather stopped, cocked her head, then started tapping her foot. Leslie recognized the tight jaw and pursed lips of irritation, having often been the recipient of it herself.

Abruptly, Heather sighed. "I suppose. Well, okay, that too. Just the one pair, though. All right, then, have fun, honey. I'll see you next weekend." She disconnected the call and threw up her hands. "I guess necessary school supplies include books, shoes, and two pairs of jeans. Not calling for permission, mind you, but forgiveness before the bill comes."

Jo stared at Heather, her expression blank. "Sounds right."

Moirin barked with laughter. "Ah, the expenses of parenthood. It doesn't end at high school."

Leslie grinned and assessed her sister's outfit. Heather wore wide-leg denim capris and an untucked khaki button-down shirt. The colors would blend well with the white and greens the rest of them had chosen. Leslie peered through the camera, shifting focus.

"Okay, settle into the loveseat. It's just cloudy enough that the window will be perfect. Heather and Jo seated, Moirin and I on the arms." She peered through the lens again, then pulled back.

"Yes, ma'am, Ms. James." Jo snapped her heels together and saluted before scrambling into position.

"Oh, did that sound like I was barking orders? Sorry. Arrange at will." She flapped her arms and waited for them to get comfortable.

After a couple of test shots, Leslie set the timer and rushed into the frame. As always, a couple of closed-eye shots, one silly expression when they were all laughing, and two great keepers.

"Thanks, guy," she said as she packed up the tripod.

"Aw, I know you love your memories," Heather said, squishing her in a bear hug. "We all love that you do it."

"So, now that the mandatory part is done, I say let's check out the village. We stopped at the market briefly, but I saw so many cute shops I'd like to investigate," Jo said.

"I could go for some shopping, especially if we get to walk outside as well," Moirin said.

"Plus, we should get more food!" Leslie said.

"Well, that settles it," Heather said, nodding. "Let's head into town."

4
SHOPPING & A RESCUE CAT

Heather backed the Pacifica out of the driveway, checking the mirrors and backup camera for low-hanging branches and woodland creatures that might be inclined to dash across her path.

Jo sat in the passenger seat, running her hands across the leather and the large display. "This is nice. I keep thinking I need to get a new car but keep putting it off."

"Thanks. Tabor chose it. He insisted I needed it. I didn't think I was going to like it, but I do." She navigated between the low-hanging tree branches, smiling at Jo as she managed to avoid all contact. It wouldn't do to scratch up her brand-new vehicle.

Leslie's voice carried the conversation from the back seat. "I'm not saying jogging is bad, but speed walking is lower impact. It's better for your knees but still good for the heart."

Heather heard Moirin grunt. "My knees are fine. Jogging builds muscle and gives a better calorie burn."

Give me a stationary bike any day. Better yet, diet food that tastes good. Heather kept that thought to herself. Otherwise, all three of them would start lecturing her.

Jo toyed with the large touch screen and zoomed in on a local map, finding a route to the center of town. She adjusted the settings, deciding on the most direct route rather than the fastest. "This way looks prettiest," she said.

Heather couldn't see any difference, except that the map was green and blue without white lines indicating housing areas. It seemed in Jo's mind that prettier was more remote.

"…core strengthening, sure. risk of injury… oh, good point." Snippets of Moirin and Leslie's back-seat debate on the benefits of jogging versus power walking floated to the front seat, but Heather tuned it out.

She followed the turns as directed, finding herself on a hilly, curvy, two-lane road behind a horse trailer being towed at forty miles an hour by a heavy-duty pickup truck with Dually wheels. Rocks from the semi-gravel road pitched at them, each clanking as it hit the hood or clinking as it collided with the windshield.

She winced. After the third missile, she eased the Pacifica into the left lane and, seeing her way clear, passed the truck.

A few miles later, she encountered a second trailer. "I haven't seen any horses in pastures around here. I wonder why so many people are hauling them around?"

"Maybe they have a rodeo going on this weekend. Oh, wouldn't that be fun?" Leslie said, leaning forward from the back seat.

"As long as I don't have to keep driving around these things," Heather mumbled as she flipped on the blinker and slid into the left lane. A hill and a curve were up ahead, blocking her vision, but there had been few other vehicles, so it was likely no one was coming. She played the odds, accelerating to pass the truck. Halfway through the maneuver, a car appeared at the top of the hill, just in front of them.

Her heart flew to her throat, and her stomach clenched. The muscles in her body locked, except for her right foot, which pressed the accelerator to the floor.

Jo inhaled sharply as the engine gunned, spitting gravel into the wheel wells. Heather's fingers tightened on the steering wheel as she cleared the truck and yanked the vehicle back into the right-hand lane. She released the breath she'd been holding, realizing the oncoming car was still a safe distance away.

"Just feel like you needed some NASCAR practice time?" Moirin's voice dripped with sarcasm.

Heather's hands shook, "I saw that car coming and I panicked. I'm not used to country roads like this. I'm sorry."

A few minutes later, her heart was still fluttering as they arrived in the village. She unclenched her fingers, still white as they still gripped the steering wheel. She slowed her speed, taking in the quaint town. It was clean, well-maintained, and welcoming, with flowers in large pots on the sidewalk and trailing from baskets hanging along light posts. Shops, small restaurants, and specialty stores lined the main street, and clusters of people strolled the sidewalks. It was lively, but not overrun with tourists.

"This place is adorable. How have we not been here before?" Jo turned her head from side to side.

"We spend too much time in Denver, I suppose," Heather said. She neared an empty parking spot, nearly stopped, then sped up again. "Which is ironic, because it's driving here that I find intimidating. I hate parallel parking, but with all these big trucks and horse trailers everywhere, how do people see around them? For that matter, how do people drive them, *and* manage to parallel park them?" She shook her head as Leslie and Moirin chuckled.

"It's okay. I hate parallel parking too. There's a parking lot on your left up there," Jo said.

Heather breathed a thankful prayer as she parked and stepped out of the vehicle. There wasn't a horse trailer in sight.

"Let's walk up the street where we drove in. There were a few places that looked interesting." Heather dug a straw hat out of a huge matching bag. She put the hat on, shielding her eyes from the sun, then slung the bag over her shoulder.

They browsed several clothing stores, a flower shop, a candle boutique, and a souvenir shop before ducking into a sandwich shop. It was well past noon, and it had been too long since the early morning muffins. Thankfully, the line was short, and soon they took their wax-paper-wrapped sandwiches to a bistro table set up on the sidewalk outside the shop.

Heather's stomach grumbled as she unwrapped the thick slices of brioche bread stuffed with seafood salad. She groaned at the first bite of soft, sweet, buttery bread and the tangy creaminess of the seafood with crunchy chopped vegetables. "Oh, this is heavenly."

Jo nodded, her mouth too full to speak, a smear of mayonnaise on the side of her cheek.

Moirin waved a napkin at Jo. "I haven't had a grinder in years, but this is as good as I've ever had."

Jo grabbed the napkin and dabbed her face. She finished the sandwich, then balled up the wax paper and leaned back in the chair, grinning with contentment."

"You guys ready?" Leslie stood, gathering the trash from their lunch. "Let's cross over at the corner and go back down the other side? There's a leather store over there I'd like to check out."

They walked a few feet when Jo's cell phone rang. She pulled it from a small case attached to her belt. "Hello? Oh, hi Kyle." *My brother,* she mouthed.

Heather slowed her steps, matching Jo's reduced pace.

"Yeah, I'm good. You?" She was silent, but flashed a smile at Heather, raising her hand to make a chatting-mouth impression. "Great, great. Hey, can I call you back maybe Sunday afternoon? I'm away with the girls for the weekend."

Jo stopped walking and laid her hand on Heather's arm. "Uh, huh. Oh. Well, no, that's not." Jo frowned and pursed her lips. "Well, maybe I could do something, but not that exactly. Hang on a sec," she said, then, lowering the phone, pressing it against her leg.

"What's up?" Heather said.

"Oh, some family thing. I'll just talk to him real quick and catch up with you guys." Jo pointed back to the café tables. "I'm going to go back and sit."

"Are you sure? I'm happy to hang out here with you."

"No, it's fine. I'm sure I won't be long, and I'll meet you guys in a few blocks." Jo turned before Heather could respond, speaking low into her phone, and she walked away.

Heather watched her friend scurry back to the table. That family always seemed to be imposing on her for one favor or another. Jo went out of her way to please them, much more than Heather would have done if their roles were reversed. She had her times of frustration with Leslie, but they knew where to draw the line.

She crossed the street and caught up with Leslie and Moirin halfway down the block. Glancing over, she saw Jo still hunched over the table. "Ugh, that woman is a saint," she mumbled as she followed the other two into the shop.

The aroma of leather, with undertones of wood, smoke, and an unfamiliar, earthy, musky scent, filled her nostrils. The front window was stuffed with cowboy paraphernalia, mostly unrecognizable to Heather. She glanced over the display and scanned the store. Nothing caught her attention.

Leslie browsed a sale rack of flowy bohemian shirts in a variety of muted earthtone colors. Any one of them would be dull and lifeless on someone else, but Leslie's tawny coloring and tall, lean figure could carry the style, elevating it to casual elegance. Heather joined her and flipped through the selection of shirts, the metal tops of the plastic hangers screeching in protest as they scraped along the metal rod. The colors and patterns blended together as they flew by. She barely noticed.

It was all the routine of window shopping and retail browsing. The fun had gone out of shopping several years ago. Her closet was full of trendy clothes, ranging from casual to classy, but she usually wore scrubs for work. Most evenings, it seemed silly to change when she was at home alone. It took long hours to be a successful surgeon at Tabor's level, and he only managed to spend the evening at home once or twice a week. She knew better than most the demands of the healthcare industry. Her own career in Physical Therapy had required years of education and practical experience. Settled into a practice now for the past few years, her schedule was reliably consistent.

A man in jeans, wearing a leather vest over a buttoned-down tan shirt, sat on a stool behind a long wooden counter. Heather couldn't help but notice the enormous square golden-tone belt buckle with elaborate designs. He leaned back on the stool as he chewed on a toothpick sticking out of his mouth, shifting it from one side to the other as he spoke. A second, taller man, also wearing jeans and a leather vest, but also sporting a straw cowboy hat, leaned on the counter, nodding.

"Help ya, hon?" The man behind the counter raised his voice a few decibels, pointing toward Leslie with his chin.

"Oh, no, thank you. I'm just looking." Leslie smiled at the two men.

"You okay? Help ya find anything special?" The proprietor looked at Moirin, who looked up and shook her head.

He assumed Heather wasn't looking to buy anything in his store. Either that, or, despite only being a couple of years older, she'd reached the point of middle-aged invisibility.

"That scarf would be real pretty with your eyes." The cowboy with the hat said, smiling at Leslie.

"What do you think? Leslie looked at Heather.

She shrugged. Fashion was more Moirin's expertise. Scrubs were easy to match every morning. Anything more complicated and she'd need a personal shopper to help.

Leslie walked to a mirror and tossed the silky scarf around her neck, flipping her hair to bring the silk against her skin. It fell perfectly in a way that would take Heather ten minutes and three YouTube videos to accomplish.

The cowboy gave a low wolf whistle and smiled at Leslie again. She blushed and pulled at one end of the scarf, letting it slide off and pool into her hand.

He winked and returned to his conversation with the proprietor. Heather stifled a smile. An attractive, grounded cowboy might just be the stabilizing influence Leslie needed in her life. Too bad this one lived several hours away from Denver.

She stepped over to the window and peered out. Seeing that Jo was still at the table across the street, she stepped outside, waiting in the shade for Leslie and Moirin to exit, wondering idly if Leslie would purchase the scarf. Maybe if the smiling cowboy offered another compliment. She seemed oblivious to the cowboy's flirting, yet was prone to impulse buys.

Leslie exited, clutching a small bag, and Moirin followed behind her with a much larger one. Heather smiled. *She bought the scarf.*

Moirin may have influenced Leslie more than the flirty cowboy. There was nothing wrong with that. Moirin was an excellent role model, and it would do Leslie good to be more like her, if somewhat less in spending. Moirin came from wealth that the Leslie and Heather could only dream about.

"It looks like there's a grocery store down the street. Should we walk down and pick up something for tonight?" Heather asked.

"That sounds good. We should refill their coffee supply as well," Moirin said. "You'll have to let us know what else we can do for our hosts to show our appreciation."

"Hey, where's Jo?" Leslie looked around, glancing back into the store and squinting.

Heather pointed across the street to where Jo sat on the bench, still holding the phone to her ear with one hand, and gesturing in the air with the other. "She's talking to one of her brothers. She said she'd catch up."

"Okay. Well, it's a small town. It's not like she'll get lost, and worst case, we'll meet back at the car," Leslie said, sliding her sunglasses on.

"I hope everything is okay. She's been talking to him a long time," Heather said.

"If it's not, we're here for her. In the meantime, let's go to the store." Moirin's voice was firm and decisive. She pulled her sunglasses down from where they rested on top of her head, then turned. "Speed walk?"

"I think I'll plod along and give Jo time to catch up." Heather dangled her fingers downward and waved her hands, shoo'ing them away, as if she were encouraging children to run to the playground.

They scurried down the sidewalk, leaving Heather to amble behind, along with others heading the same direction. She enjoyed the leisurely walk, still concerned that Jo hadn't joined them yet. As she arrived at the store, a farmers' market was set up in the parking lot. Throngs of people milled around the tents and tables, talking with vendors and examining goods for sale. The air was filled with the competing scents of smoked meats, flowers, scented soaps, and sugar.

She spotted Moirin at one of the first booths in the center, where she was perusing organic honey and hand-blended spices. Heather joined her, accepting the butternut squash ginger cookie the vendor offered.

"Where's Leslie?" Heather asked, looking around at the adjoining booths.

"She wanted to do the grocery shopping while I browsed here. You know how Jo loves to cook, and it's never too early to start Christmas shopping."

Heather laughed. "You mean you're not stocking your kitchen with exotic spices and a crazy-looking rolling pin?"

"Ha. You know me better than that. You and I would split second place if we were the only entrants in a toast-making competition." Moirin pulled the rolling pin from under her arm. "And this lovely item is Norwegian. The detail is called rosemaling. The rolling pin imprints this intricate pattern on dough. I thought Jo would love it."

Heather examined the craftsmanship. "It is lovely," she said, handing it back.

"Well, I'm done here, I think. Should we check on Leslie?" Moirin nodded to the vendor as she left, Heather following.

The last booth at the corner had a large sign encouraging adoptions and donations to the local animal shelter. Heather shivered. Most animals of the domestic house-pet variety were, at best, dirty and noisy. At their worst, they were terrifying and dangerous, as unpredictable as livestock and beasts in the wild. She cautiously stepped around Moirin to walk on the outside, leaving her friend as a buffer to the potentially vicious creatures.

As they passed, a long-haired chocolate-and-ivory-colored cat stared at them intently with bright blue eyes that seemed too intelligent to be natural. Her stomach churned, and her heart jumped as Moirin turned and reached down.

"Don't," she couldn't contain the warning before it croaked from her mouth.

Moirin smiled as she reached down and stroked the animal. Heather took a half-step backward, as Moirin murmured to the cat. From that safe distance, Heather could appreciate the beauty of the animal, which had obviously survived major injuries. He had missing patches of fur on his back, near his chocolate-colored tail, and the back of his right leg. It seemed to limp as it walked back and forth under Moirin's hand.

"He must sense that you're quite a cat-lover. I've never seen Orson respond to anyone like that." A young man wearing a red t-shirt with "Furry Friends Animal Rescue Volunteer" printed across the front stood by the cat on the other side of the table. He looked at Moirin with an expression of amazement and respect.

"Orson?"

"Yes, that's his name. He's a Birman. It's a beautiful breed, and normally very social, but this guy's had a tough time this year. He shies away from people till he susses them out."

"He looks like he's had some injuries. Do you know what happened?" Heather edged closer as Moirin stroked Orson's ears.

"He came to us this past winter in bad shape. Seemed like a wild animal may have gotten him. He was chipped, but turns out his owner died, so we took him in. He's been recuperating about six months and the doc said he's ready for a forever home." The volunteer looked at Moirin, his eyes hopeful. "But he seems to have bonded with you. Are you looking to adopt?"

"I've never considered having a pet. And I work a lot, so it doesn't seem fair."

"That's something to think about. Birmans are social and don't like being left alone for long periods. But they're smart, pretty calm, and he would do well in an apartment," the volunteer said, glancing at Heather and nodding, as if encouraging her support. "They like their humans, and the companionship is great for single people or families with children."

Heather stepped beside Moirin. "He does seem to like you. Maybe you *should* have a pet. You seem to like him, and he looks like he could use a break in life. I think Orson here might be just what you need."

It must be sad to come home to a quiet, empty house at night. The nights since Camilla was gone, when Tabor was working late, gave Heather an uncomfortable insight into Moirin's life, and she was happy she wasn't in the same situation, being single at fifty years old. A wave of guilt followed the thought.

But then, Moirin had always been the strong one of the group, but she never had the opportunity to balance marriage and children with her career. Her family owned a huge energy company that Moirin had turned into an international conglomerate. She was a high-powered executive handling billions of dollars and making a profound impact on the world in ways the rest of them could barely comprehend.

Sometimes Heather was jealous of the glamorous lifestyle, but mostly she felt sorry for her. She seemed lonely, frazzled, and overworked, trying to meet everyone's expectations of her. Maybe a cat would help ground her and give her something to love that wouldn't leave.

Orson meowed.

Moirin hesitated, then nodded. "There's something about him. I don't think I can say no."

"He seems like he's already decided you're his human. I think you have to go with it. You'll make it work."

"Yeah, I will," Moirin said, scooping Orson into her arms. "You and me, buddy."

Heather gave a thumbs up to the volunteer, who beamed.

"I'll get some paperwork and everything you'll need," he said. "I have a feeling this will be a perfect match."

5
DINNER IN THE VILLAGE

Jo slouched on a bench in front of the parking lot, Heather's Pacifica in her line of sight. She didn't feel much like shopping, and it was too hot to wander around looking for them. Sooner or later, they'd return to the car.

She looked down at her phone, the eBook reader application open to a novel she was trying to finish. Her attention kept wandering. As much as she tried to resist, the knot in her stomach twisted and turned, pulling her into a vortex of anxiety. All she wanted this weekend was peace. If she had just let the call go to voicemail, she could have avoided all this.

A cat mewed pitifully, stretching its complaint into a yowl.

Jo turned and felt her mouth drop open, feeling for a moment like a shocked cartoon character. A giggle bubbled in her chest, and she burst out laughing.

Heather walked toward her, carrying a large shopping bag and several smaller ones. Leslie was a few steps behind, her arms loaded with shopping bags, a long loaf of Italian bread sticking out from the top of one. Most incongruous was Moirin, red-faced, shuffling behind Leslie with several lumpy-looking canvas bags over one shoulder, and a huge cat carrier, visibly heavy as she held on with both hands, duck-walking around the burden. A tawny-colored, fluffy tail stuck out from the grated front.

She had never seen Moirin looking more inelegant or awkward. Swallowing her mirth, Jo rushed to help. "What in the world is all of this?" She pulled the bags from Moirin's shoulder, peering down at the carrier.

Moirin wheezed and stopped to catch her breath. "I guess you could call it an impulse buy. Or impulse adoption would be more apt. This is Orson." She lifted the carrier slightly in introduction.

Jo raised an eyebrow. Moirin was more of a researcher, planner, and checklist maker. The last impulsive thing she could remember Moirin doing was pulling in after seeing a wine tasting sign and ending up buying a case of wine. She shrugged. "Okay. This is fun."

They walked to the SUV, stowing the bags and cat carrier in the back. Jo looked at the weary trio and decided they should take the most direct route back to the house, setting the instructions into the GPS. Ten minutes later, she helped them carry the miscellaneous sacks and bags into the house.

Heather and Leslie disappeared upstairs while Moirin took her new feline companion to the garage, hoping to find a safe place to settle him for the night.

Jo grunted, heaving the grocery bags on the kitchen counter. The anxiety that swelled inside before had subsided, but she was drained. Her mind searched for a calming church chorus, something that usually brought peace. *Be strong and courageous. Do not be frightened, and do not be dismayed,* her mind recalled the Old Testament verse as she hummed them tunelessly under her breath.

Her movements felt mechanical as she unpacked the groceries. She set the loaf of Italian bread on the counter, then placed two boxes of flavored snack crackers and a package of hummus, along with a large container of mild roast coffee, in the first bag. The second contained a dozen frosted cinnamon rolls from the store bakery, a prepackaged bag of garden salad, and a family-size box of frozen lasagna.

Jo groaned. The calorie count in one serving of these things was insane, not to mention the carbs and cholesterol. She flipped the package over. Of course, it would have microwave instructions. Processed, chemical-filled convenience junk food is all that was. *What had Leslie been thinking?* She spun, opened the freezer, and tossed the offensive box inside.

That was unkind. Jo exhaled, counting to ten. *You're thoughtless and selfish, Jo. You always have been. Always acting like a goodie two-shoes, but always when it really counts, you're selfish.* Her brother's accusations echoed in her mind. Guilt came in waves from the pit of her stomach until it formed a throbbing lump in her throat. *This wasn't fair.* Oh, there it is now, the whiny victim. That's an effective response. She chided herself, and she took a deep breath, pushing down the desire to cry.

She stood, facing the refrigerator, cooling her palms and forehead on its smooth surface. They were going to need dinner soon. Either she'd need to heat the lasagna or find something else to make. It was best to focus on something productive.

"Hey, are you okay?"

Jo flinched, hearing Heather's voice as a hand touched her shoulder. "You startled me."

"What's wrong?"

"What? Oh, nothing. Just lost in thought." She forced a laugh, the gritty noise sounding false, even to her own ears.

Heather tugged at Jo's elbow, leading her to a chair at the island. "You're a lousy liar, girlfriend. Plus, your nose always gets red on the end when you're trying not to be emotional."

Jo dropped her arms on the counter, laying her head between them, and linked her fingers behind her neck. "I'm just tired," she mumbled.

"Let's see," Heather cleared her throat and used her no-nonsense mom voice. Jo chuckled, thinking of all the times they'd ribbed her for it when she'd used that tone with Camilla over the phone. Leslie said she bet it came in handy, too, for Heather to motivate someone through painful physical therapy. Jo pulled her head up, propping it against her hand, facing Heather for her *talking-to*. "You made us all muffins this morning, we had a nice coffee, you smiled for all the photos, and we had a nice lunch. You got a phone call and have been a Debbie-Downer ever since. So, what did your brother say this time to make you feel awful?"

"He didn't," Jo said.

"Aht, aht, aht." Heather shook her finger, interrupting her protest. "Both of your stepbrothers specialize in taking advantage of your kindness and good nature. They bully you and gaslight you into thinking you owe them, and I swear they enjoy making you feel bad about imaginary things."

"I just need to think it through. He just surprised me, and maybe he's right, but I don't know."

"Tell me about it." She folded her hands on the countertop, patiently waiting.

"I love my family, I'm grateful for them, and I truly enjoy helping them. I don't mean to be selfish, but sometimes, they just ask a lot." Jo's lower lip quivered, and she twisted her expression into a smile.

Heather had seen for years the evidence of Jo's soft-heartedness and sacrifice. Even now, she seemed to be blaming herself. "You're one of the least selfish people I know, honey. That's for certain."

"Kyle says that my parents are having a hard time with money. But, everyone's struggling, right? Still, Kyle said that Kevin offered to split the shortfall with me," Jo said.

Heather frowned. "Have you looked at their budget?"

Jo shook her head. "Kyle told me they want to keep it private. I know they had investments, retirement funds, and both draw social security."

"It doesn't seem right to ask for money but refuse to share the budget. If it were me, I'd insist on that. You don't know if there's really a need or not. It's Kyle asking, not your parents."

"True, but I wouldn't want to embarrass them."

Heather grasped Jo's hand. "You are as much one of their children as the rest. Parenting isn't about blood. You have a family bond, and it's okay to talk to them about finances and budgeting before you give them money. You and Kevin should talk to them together. And you shouldn't feel like having that conversation locks you into anything. Kyle's older than you. He shouldn't be throwing the responsibility off on you anyway."

"Yes, but.."

"But nothing. It's like we talked about last night. Being constantly at odds is not productive. You're trying to get back on your feet financially. You have to be honest with them about that, and if they truly need help, they have to be honest with you about that. Without Kyle guilt-tripping you into anything."

"He'll be upset, though."

"Let him," Heather said firmly. "He'll get over it. You can take care of your family, but you have to look out for your own interests first. You can't draw from a dry well."

Jo smiled and stood up, brushing her hands together. "I like that. I should put that on a pillow. Of course, you're right. Anyway, it's not an issue for right now Enough of being a Gloomy-Gus. I'll preheat the oven and get that lasagna cooked."

"When did you have time to make a lasagna? Girl, you spoil us," Heather said, shaking her head.

"Oh, not to disappoint you, but Leslie bought a frozen one at the store. I don't have any other ingredients, so we don't have much choice." Jo hunched her shoulders and wrinkled up her nose. It wasn't something she was looking forward to eating, and Heather seemed to agree.

"Ew, no way. The owners here can keep that for emergency food during the apocalypse. Plus, we don't need you to be cooking for all of us. We're all here to relax and have a nice weekend together. There are plenty of restaurants in town. We're going out."

Ninety minutes later, they were seated at a steakhouse, surrounded by the aroma of grilled beef and fresh bread.

Jo leaned close to Heather. "Thank you. I'm so glad you suggested it."

"Of course. Seems like you've got some stuff going on." Heather cocked her head and frowned. "I still think you should share."

"Maybe later. I'm feeling better about all of it," Jo said.

"And for you?" A server appeared between them.

"Yes," Heather said, patting Jo's hand before glancing down at her menu. "Prime rib, please, garlic mashed, and mixed vegetables."

"I'll have a sirloin, medium rare, baked potato loaded, and the house salad," Jo said when the server looked at her, eyebrows raised in silent question.

"I still can't believe you adopted a cat, Moirin," Leslie said. "He's so pretty. I never imagined you with any kind of pet, but somehow it matches you."

Moirin laughed. "It's just a little crazy. I tell you, when he looked at me with those intelligent, pretty blue eyes, I knew he would be the best listener. I'll scratch his ears and tell him all about my day. We're already buddies. And you guys were worried I couldn't commit." She smiled as she reached toward the center of the table and plucked a piece of bread from the basket, setting it on her side plate to butter.

Jo exchanged a long look with Heather. A thousand thoughts ran through her head before she settled on the most innocuous. "I think it's wonderful. It's about time you had someone at home you can share all the work stress with and all your super-confidential secrets."

"You might be right," Moirin said. There are some things I can't talk to anyone about, so I end up talking to myself at home. I might feel less crazy talking to a cat."

The table was silent for a second, then they all burst out laughing.

"Okay, yes, I heard it as soon as the words were out of my mouth." Moirin blushed and took a drink of her water.

Jo chuckled. Two servers came to the table, one with drinks and the other with salads. They all waited for the dishes and glasses of wine to be placed before them before continuing their conversation.

"You know you can talk to us about anything," Heather said to Moirin, then switched her gaze to Jo. "I know we all keep each other's confidence, one hundred percent."

"I appreciate that, truly," Moirin said. "And I do take advantage of that for some things. I have this board restructuring that's hanging over me right now, and I appreciate being able to talk it out."

"I'm happy to listen, but I don't know anything about your board or how to help you," Leslie said, shrugging as she picked at her salad.

"Exactly. You don't have any vested interest, so you won't try to pressure me one way or the other. It just helps to talk things out, and you all are very good at finding flaws in logic."

"Here! Here!" Jo said, offering up her wineglass. They all raised their glasses and toasted.

Heather listened, chewing on her salad, as Moirin talked about several members of the board stepping down. She wanted to focus on more green initiatives and renewable energy sources and needed a younger board.

"You know, this sort of reminds me of advice our grandmother said her mother gave her. Ok, yes, so that makes it really old-fashioned, but I think it's relevant." Heather set her fork on her plate and rested an elbow on the table. "It was actually marriage advice, but still. She said, *start as you mean to go on*. That makes sense. You can't start a thing one way, then change midstream and expect it to be smooth. If you want to move away from a traditional energy business model, it will be tougher will all the same people who are committed to the traditional way. You have to have fresh thinkers."

"Exactly my thoughts. Uncle Ian and Dad have been successful with coal, oil, and natural gas, and the company has shared interest in a couple of nuclear plants, all very profitable, and they're happy with that. I'm not against profits but I'd like to pursue alternatives with less environmental impact. If I restructure the board now, we can move more in that direction and it will be a good foundation for when I take over as CEO."

"Can you do that?" Jo asked.

"It will be a marked change for me. I've always followed Dad and Uncle Ian's lead, but to do this, I'll need to persuade my Dad and exert some influence on a few others. I'd be actively promoting my own agenda for the first time." Jo could detect the unusual mix of consternation and excitement in Moirin's voice.

"I admire how dedicated you are to the environment. If more people in the energy sector thought like you, maybe things would be better," Heather said.

Jo agreed. But it was brave too. She wished she had Moirin's bravery. After all these years, she still couldn't bear to stand up to her own relatives. She couldn't risk it. Without them, who would she have? She'd lost enough in life already.

"What do you think, Jo?" Leslie waved her hand, palm up, in the air, waiting for an answer. "It looked like you were miles away."

"I'm sorry, I guess I was. What was the question?"

"She asked your opinion about mixing art class with history lesson for her second graders," Moirin said. "But I think we'd all rather know what's going on with you. You've been odd since this afternoon."

She missed quite a bit of the conversation. Jo looked at Heather, who nodded. It would be easier to share since she'd already unburdened herself once today.

She sighed. "Fine. Yes, Kyle called this afternoon. You know he can be difficult. It just took me by surprise, and I'm not sure what to do."

"Okay." Leslie sat back and folded her arms. "What is it he wants you to do?"

"It's about money," Jo said, taking a stab at her potato.

"Isn't it always?" Moirin snorted.

"Well, maybe this time he's right, maybe," Jo said. "You all know I sold that building. He says my parents are having financial trouble and asked me to cover part of their monthly expenses for a while. It's reasonable, since I have a little extra."

"Wait a minute. Yesterday, you said you were relieved to sell the building because your savings were pretty low. You just started a new job. If anything happens to that, or you have some unexpected expenses. I think you need to bank that money and hold onto it." Leslie tapped her finger on the table as she spoke, a thump emphasizing each word.

"I have to agree with Leslie, here," Moirin said. "You know me, I'm completely committed to family, but you have to take care of yourself first. Besides that, I think your brothers, your sister, too, for that matter, should be pitching in before they come to you. They're blood relatives after all."

A familiar stab of pain went through Jo's chest. Moirin was right. Kevin and Kyle were her stepdad's sons. Ariel was their biological daughter, born after they married. Jo was just a leftover responsibility from Cindy's first marriage to Jo's father before he died. The only member of the family with a different last name, as she was often reminded of in childhood. After all these years, they were just family. Last names shouldn't matter anymore. But she still owed a debt of loyalty and responsibility, didn't she? She sipped her wine.

Besides, she had asked Kyle that same question this afternoon. His response wasn't unexpected. *C'mon, Jo, I've got three kids, Kevin's got two, and Ariel's pregnant. We've all got a lot of expenses, and you've got no mortgage and no kids. It's family, Jo, and you have more to spare, so you should give more.*

"Blood or not, aren't family the ones you're supposed to count on?" Jo looked from Heather to Jo and back to Moirin. "I feel like I'm obligated to help. It just seems selfish not to."

"I understand how you feel, Jo. But I don't think it's just a choice between give money or don't give money," Heather said, then looked around the table. "I told her earlier to look at their budget. Maybe she could see where the money's going and help them rebalance expenses."

"That's an excellent idea," Moirin said, nodding before taking the final bite of her steak. "Oh, I love a good meal and a round of problem-solving. It's like everything is right with the world."

Jo laughed, feeling lighter and fortunate to have these friends. The thought of her next conversation with Kyle didn't bring a twist of anxiety to her gut. After working through her own financial nightmare, Leslie was right; she didn't want to go back to worrying about a shrinking nest egg. Heather's solution might work. It was worth pursuing.

"This kind of thing should teach us all a lesson," Heather said. "One day, we're going to be in our seventies, and we'll need to take care of ourselves. Physically and financially. Tabor and I are empty-nesters now, and we'll be doing more things together, but we still need to keep up that savings. Running out of money is a scary thought." Heather frowned and drained the last of her wine from the glass.

She wondered if it was too late to find someone to spend her old age with. Looking at Moirin, she smiled. At least her friend had a cat now for company.

6
SATURDAY NIGHT FIREPIT CHAT

It was fully dark with the sky filled with twinkling stars when they arrived back at the house. The air was still and much cooler than it had been during the day. They changed into jeans and sweatshirts to hang out on their second and final night.

"Next getaway needs to be at least a three-day weekend. This has been great, but I think I need more than forty-eight hours," Jo said, curling her feet up on the wicker loveseat.

"I second that," Leslie said as she fiddled with the dials and buttons on the propane-powered firepit. A click, the *whoooosh* as the fire licked over the square of lava rocks.

Heather, Jo, and Moirin applauded. "Always the clever mechanical one," Heather cheered. She sat down across from Jo in a wicker chair with plush cushions.

"That's why you should always have a teacher with you. We're the best at reading instructions." Leslie dragged a chair in front of the fire pit, between Jo and Heather. She sat down, drawing up her knees and wrapping her hands around them.

The night air was filled with the chirping of insects, the occasional deep hoot of an owl, and a few whirls and clicks of other forest-dwellers.

"I have two bottles here," Moirin said, holding them up. They're new blends from Aunt Aggie's winery. I knew you'd want to taste-test." She opened the first bottle and poured three glasses, handing one to Heather and another to Jo, keeping the third for herself. She handed Leslie a glass of lemonade before taking the seat across from her.

"How's Aggie doing? I haven't seen her in so long." Jo sipped the wine, then smacked her lips. "Very nice."

"I went up a few weeks ago. She's doing well. Happy that things are picking up and getting back to normal again."

"That's good to hear. We should take a Saturday sometime and go see her," Jo said.

"Oh, I'd love that," Leslie said, looking at Heather, who nodded.

"I love her insights on life. She's the only other woman I know who was widowed early in life and pursued her dreams. I find that so inspirational. Plus, she makes great wine." Jo held up her glass in salute before taking another sip, then setting the glass on the table next to her.

"You've done a good job of that, I think," Leslie said. "You seem happy in this stage of life. Getting rid of that building was a responsible decision. And now you're jazzed about finally using your degree. I'm excited for you. Just be strong with this family stuff."

"Thank you for all the encouragement. I feel so much better about the sale and the money. Honestly, having a cushion in the bank again is such a relief." Jo smiled at Leslie.

"To embracing your dreams!" Moirin lifted her glass in a toast.

"To finding your path." Heather echoed Moirin's sentiment, raising her glass in a toast of her own.

"To very happy birthdays, Heather and Moirin," Jo said.

"Thank you," Moirin said, taking a long sip from the glass.

Leslie stared at the fire, aware that the others had also fallen silent in private contemplation. The silence didn't last long. Soon, the sounds of the night forest surrounded them. The cricket chirping seemed loudest, but she could discern the rhythmic lapping of waves at the lake and scurrying of small creatures through the leaves and underbrush. A high-pitched, piercing bugle rang out, seeming to reverberate in the air.

Heather sat up, planting her feet on the deck, her eyes wide as she swiveled her head, trying to pinpoint the sound. "Was that a wolf? Do you think we're safe here?"

"We're fine. I've heard that before up at Aunt Aggie's place. It's just an elk."

Leslie stood up and put an arm around her sister's shoulder. "It's okay. We're safe here. Sit and enjoy this. It's so regal. If we're lucky, we might hear wolves or coyotes. It's all part of the adventure in the great outdoors."

"Of course." Heather shrugged and sat down, holding her body erect as if keeping ready for a flight-or-fight moment.

"You should get used to new adventures and experiences," Moirin said. "With Camilla off to college full-time now, you and Tabor are going to be official empty-nesters. You'll have a lot more time on your hands."

"That's true. She'll probably still come by with laundry or something." Heather laughed, settling back in her chair. "We know for sure she won't stop by for a home-cooked meal. Unless she misses how I stash diced broccoli in the macaroni and cheese. It was almost gourmet. I always use the kind with cheese packet and not the dry stuff."

Jo rolled her eyes and groaned. "Okay, enough. Maybe I should come over once a week so I can give you cooking lessons."

"That's not a bad idea," Leslie said. "I've been reading about turning fifty, and how it's your third act in life, so you need to try new things and learn stuff. You know, childhood, then adulthood, and now whatever this stage is called. It's not retirement yet, but working that way I guess. But, activity really good for your brain as you age. And for relationships, too. I have some articles to send you all about romance and rekindling intimacy. It says you should spend quality time together doing stuff like date nights, starting new hobbies together, and traveling more."

"Stop, stop." Heather held her hands up in front of her face. "I can't have my sister talking to me about rekindling intimacy with my husband."

Moirin laughed. "Well, she has a point. I've read a few articles about life transitions, but I'm looking for ways to help my dad find interests that take him out of the office. He's supposed to be retired already and only involved at Garrett as Chairman of the Board, but he still comes in several times a week to check on things. They say you should look to childhood interests and rekindle them, but that hasn't worked yet."

"Oh, so maybe the workaholic gene runs in the family," Leslie said, snickering. "Maybe you should look into cultivating a few more interests yourself."

"I have plenty of interests, thank you very much. We're talking about Heather."

"Heather is just fine, thanks," Heather said as she stood and turned her wineglass upside down, letting the last two drops fall on the deck. "Who else needs a refill?" She topped off Lelie's glass with the remains from the pitcher and refilled the rest of the glasses with the second blend Moirin brought.

They had a lively discussion on the merits of each, and in the end, declared both to be worth of stocking.

"So, Leslie, will you be teaching at the same school that your boys attend?" Moirin asked.

"No, I'm back in the north suburbs, and Martin's moved the boys out to Golden." She ran her fingertip along the edge of her lemonade glass before setting it down. "He has a nice house there, I hear, with a big yard, and his job is close by, so it's working out well."

"Really? I didn't know. I'm happy you guys have stayed in touch," Jo said. "Are things getting any better with Martin?"

"Are you guys talking again?" Heather spoke over Jo as she leaned forward, resting her forearms on her thighs, clasping her hands together.

Leslie shook her head. "No. He still can't stand me, and probably would never speak to me again if it weren't for the boys. But Jean's always liked me, and she's bridging the gap. I think she talks to Martin, and maybe he listens. She makes sure the boys know I love them. She doesn't think they're ready to have me back in their lives just yet, but maybe soon."

"Does Martin know his mother keeps in touch?" Heather raised her eyebrow.

Leslie nodded. "We talk every week or two, and she tells me what's going on in their lives. Sometimes, she just calls to check on me."

"Well, they're growing up and understand things better now. Maddox would be what, twelve, now?"

"Yes. They're both going to be in middle school now. Lucas is starting sixth grade, and Maddox seventh," Leslie said. "I worry that since they spend all their time with their dad, they're getting used to me not being around. In time, they won't need me or even want me."

"That's just silly. You're their mom. They are always going to need you." Jo said. "There's a lot of hurt to get over right now. You need to accept that things will never be the way they used to be. That relationship, the four of you as a family together, that's gone, honey. The divorce is final. You just have to wait and see what a family of you and the boys looks like." Several staccato high-pitched hoots echoed in the trees nearby.

"You're lucky Martin wants you back in their lives eventually. Lots of fathers would be fighting you on that," Heather said, shivering.

"Just an owl," Jo whispered, leaning toward Heather.

"I don't know for sure that things will work out that way. He says it depends somewhat on me, but the boys have a big say in it. They may not trust me anymore. Sometimes I'm not certain I deserve that trust," Leslie said.

"Heather's right. Life changes, and you just have to do your best to prepare for them. We're all human and we make mistakes. I don't like to think about whether we deserve things, good or bad. All I know is that when we get another chance, we should accept it with grace and do our best not to repeat our mistakes," Moirin said.

"Nobody inherently knows how to be a good parent. You do your best and just try to think about how you would want to be treated. All things heal eventually, right? It's like physical therapy. Sometimes, the healing phase is more painful than the injury itself. But you've got to complete the healing process."

Leslie moaned, letting her head fall back. The stars twinkled in the pitch-black sky. "I'm much better at *find it, fix it*. Patience is a virtue that's still a work in progress for me."

"You'll get there. You're on the right path." Jo yawned. "But right now, I think I need to be on the path of sleep."

"Me too. I'm going to call it a night." Heather stood up and stretched.

"Since you cleaned up last night, I'll take care of it tonight. I want to check on Orson one last time before I head upstairs," Moirin said.

"See you in the morning." Leslie hugged Moirin and followed the others upstairs.

7
SUNDAY MORNING BRUNCH

Heather sat, enveloped in silence as the sun inched its way into the day. She poured the day's first cup of coffee in the dark and watched the sky above the lake turn from inky purple to deep red, then orange and golden yellow, the sun's reflection now shimmering off the water's surface. It was really quite stunning. When had she stopped appreciating the little things in life? *Maybe I've never appreciated them because I've never taken time to stop and see them.*

She loved her life. She was a successful physical therapist, and the work was rewarding. As Camilla's mom and Tabor's wife, she had the family happiness and security she'd always wanted. But she had gone straight from years of college to long hours building a career, then longer days balancing motherhood and career. When had there ever been a time to appreciate the little things in life?

A narrow beam of light illuminated the table, just beyond where she sat, settling on the centerpiece of flowers in a glass tube. Tiny pillars of dust motes danced in the box of sunshine. It was mesmerizing until a cloud drifted and the beam disappeared.

The chair made an ugly scratching noise on the hardwood floor as she shifted it back. She walked into the kitchen, one hand gripping her coffee mug, the other running across the countertops and appliance fronts as she passed. One surface rough and warm, the next smooth and cold. The plastic handle of the coffeepot molded to her fingers and the heat rose from the pot, bringing the warmth with the bitter bold scent of dark roast to her nostrils. She turned and leaned against the counter, sipping the strong coffee.

It was quiet in the house now. Moirin had left some time before, dressing in jogging clothes, waving wordlessly as she headed out the door. She should get used to this. Tabor rarely sat enjoying morning coffee. To be honest, she rarely had either. Weekday mornings were a rush to the clinic, weekends an endless to-do list of laundry, cleaning, and shopping for one thing or another. If she didn't have those tasks, what would she do with all the free time? If only she could try Moirin's advice of rekindling childhood hobbies. Too bad she didn't have any back then either.

It wasn't her fault. It was just life circumstances that made childhood pass her by. Grandma took them in every time Mom went to rehab, but Heather ended up looking after herself and Leslie. Grandma tried, but she worked two jobs, and after the challenges of raising her own daughter, she didn't seem to have the energy to care for two more little girls. They had the basics of shelter and clothing. Food was hit or miss. They ate a lot of canned food and boxed meals. It was no surprise that it was the cooking default for both of them, even now.

At the thought of food, her stomach growled. The coffee was going to trigger miserable heartburn if she didn't eat something. The muffins Jo had made were gone, but the cinnamon rolls still sat on the counter unopened. Heather rummaged through the drawers for a knife and slit open the cellophane wrapping. After pulling a roll away from the rest, she slid it on a plate and microwaved it for a few seconds to warm it.

The low whirl of the microwave seemed deafening in the silence. She needed to get used to the quiet. This would be her life now unless she found some new hobbies. Tabor worked long hours and was at the height of his career. It would likely be another fifteen or twenty years before he slowed down.

Fifteen or twenty years was a long time. Twenty years ago, Camilla had been a toddler. It was disconcerting to think of that much time still stretching out in front of her. *And that was just to get to retirement.* They'd likely have another ten after that. The microwave beeped.

She settled back at the table with her coffee and roll, and the front door opened. A few steps of sharp clicking heels, then two thumps. She chuckled, knowing the sound well. Tired, achy feet kicking shoes off in the only rebellion they were allowed. She turned as Jo padded across the floor barefoot, her floral sundress swishing at her knees.

"I thought you were still sleeping. Where are you coming from, all dressed up?" Heather asked.

Jo grabbed a cup from the cupboard and filled it with coffee. After taking a cautious sip, she grinned. "Cowboy church."

"Like church for cowboys? What is that?" Heather wasn't sure if she was joking. Jo's face was somber, but her eyes sparkled.

"It was sort of like church at home, but more informal. Smaller." Jo tapped her chin with one finger and closed one eye, wrinkling up her face. "It wasn't like a formal sermon, but a relatable talk, you know?"

Heather laughed. "Uh, no, I don't know. I've never gone to church. Actually, I didn't know you did either."

"I saw a flyer yesterday in one of the store windows. All the time I sat there talking to Kyle, I was staring at it. I woke up this morning and had the urge to go. I guess I just wanted to see what cowboy church was like." Jo took a step closer, leaning down to squint at Heather's plate. "Ew, what is that?"

"Cinnamon roll."

"A plateful of empty calories that probably isn't that tasty."

Heather snagged a small piece with her fork and took a bite. The sickeningly sweet frosting has run down and congealed with the sugary cinnamon filling, making a gooey sludge between the flavorless bread layers. Heather put her hand up and swung in a 'so-so' motion.

"Uh-huh. That's what I thought." Jo grabbed the plate and emptied it into the trash. "Let's make something edible. Come be my helper."

Jo dug into a plastic grocery bag on the counter and pulled out a package of turkey bacon. "You can do this," she said, pointing to the bacon. "Could you find a baking sheet and foil?"

Not waiting for an answer, she turned and rummaged through the cabinets, pulling out bowls, measuring cups and spoons, and a few pantry items. She removed a carton of eggs and a pint of milk from the grocery sack, then balled it up and threw it in the trash.

"Hey, didn't you see the recycling?" Moirin's voice startled them. Heather shrieked, and Jo dropped an egg on the countertop.

Moirin laughed as she walked over and plucked the plastic from the trash can. She scoffed, then dug out two cardboard boxes and a plastic bottle. "There's a recycling bin in the garage, guys. You know better."

Heather snickered when Jo flicked the kitchen towel at Moirin before mopping up the egg yolk that dripped on the floor. "About gave me a heart attack," Jo mumbled.

"I'm going to let Orson out for a bit, then go shower," Moirin said as she headed to the garage with the recycling.

"Well, now the kitchen officially looks like I've been cooking," Heather said, "what's next?"

Jo talked her through lining the sheet with foil and laying out the bacon before sliding it into the oven. A cold oven, Jo instructed. Set the temperature, then the timer.

"Trust me, you're going to love it. And much easier than in a frying pan, splattering grease all over the kitchen." Jo slapped her hands together, sending a while cloud of flour dust into the air.

Heather inched over and peered over her shoulder. Jo pointed at one bowl, then the other.

"Dry ingredients in here: flour, sugar, baking powder, baking soda, salt, and powder form buttermilk. That one is the eggs, added melted butter and water. That's the liquid. If you use liquid buttermilk, it takes the place of the water. We keep them separate until we're ready to make the pancakes and blend 'em once the griddle is hot. It's an old farmer's almanac pancake recipe. There's nothing better."

"Were you serious about teaching me to cook like this? I'd love to be able to make a dinner that didn't start with a can or a box." She laughed. Maybe she could start eating healthier if she prepared food from scratch.

"Of course," Jo said, rolling up the towel to keep the smeared egg inside and wiping her hands on the exterior. She spun around. "Oh, in exchange, you can teach me more about stretching exercises for sports. I read you should do that. I've been wanting to try pickleball, but I don't want to get hurt. We all saw what Leslie went through after her accident. I've heard lots of stories about women over fifty getting awful knee injuries from sports."

"I absolutely will. Even if you don't give me cooking classes in exchange." Heather still carried guilt about Leslie's struggle. She should have overseen her sister's physical therapy personally. Or, maybe if she had been around more, she would have recognized the spiral and could have stepped in. She had been too involved in her own little family, working to advance her career while being a good surgeon's wife and the best mother she knew how to be. Helping with science fair, attending volleyball games, and cheerleading practice all seemed petty and unimportant in hindsight.

At least she had done a few things right. She insisted that Leslie follow her to college, ensuring her sister secured all the scholarships and loans she needed to earn a degree. She refused to allow either of them to follow the path of their mother and grandmother. Everything had been fine until Leslie tore her knee up and couldn't wean herself off the painkillers after the surgery. A random slip on the ice changed her life forever. Leslie had admitted later that she rushed the recovery with two small boys at home to take care of and thought it was the right decision. Instead, she ended up in a dark spiral that ended her marriage and left the two boys hurt and angry, refusing to see her.

"Are you okay?"

"What? Yes, sorry. Of course, I'll show you some stretches. So, what now?"

Jo smiled and dug into the refrigerator, handing Heather an orange, some blueberries, and a few strawberries. Jo directed Heather to peel the orange while she washed the other fruits, then hulled the strawberries. She threw all of it into the blender for a minute, then dumped it into a small saucepan, adding a spoonful of honey and a dash of vanilla.

"Don't you measure when you cook?" Heather was impressed by her confidence.

Jo shrugged. "Sure, sometimes. Especially when I'm following a recipe. I'm just making a little compote to go with the pancakes since we don't have syrup. It's basic, and pretty forgiving."

The smoky scent of bacon mixed with the spicy citrus of the orange filled the kitchen. It blended with the coffee for a warm, cozy feeling. This is what she wanted in her house. Aromas that made a house feel like home. Her stomach growled.

"This is nice, Jo. Thank you."

Jo pulled another bowl down from the cabinet and set it on the counter. "I know. There's something about being in the kitchen. Maybe it's the process, or the smells, maybe the food itself. I don't know, but it feels productive and peaceful, I guess. It's like, it's grounding."

"Hmm. Maybe that's why they call the kitchen the heart of the home."

"Could be." Jo nodded as she cracked eggs into the bowl, adding a dribble of olive oil, then salt and pepper before whisking.

"I like it." Heather imagined evenings this winter with Tabor. Sitting at a table with candles, just the two of them, enjoying a dinner she'd prepared. Leslie's words echoed. A candle-lit dinner at home was a good start for reconnecting. They'd had a romantic connection once, before life became a partnership of accomplishing tasks and errands. *How long had it been since they'd truly enjoyed each other's company?* She couldn't remember the last time they'd laughed together, and she had to admit it had been months since they'd been intimate. For years, she and Tabor had only a child and a life routine in common. But then, neither of them had hobbies or any true outside interests. His weekly golf game was more for professional connections than pleasure.

Footsteps thundered on the stairs. A moment later, Leslie burst into the kitchen. "Good morning, my beauties. Isn't it a perfect day?"

"That it is." Heather smiled at Leslie. Her face was glowing, looking happy and healthy. "Why don't you set the table. I think Moirin will be down in a minute."

Leslie nodded and bounded between the kitchen and dining room, ducking around Jo and Heather as she grabbed glasses, silverware, and plates. Heather loaded the bacon onto a platter and started another pot of coffee while Jo flipped pancakes and scrambled eggs.

By the time Moirin came down, freshly showered and dressed, the meal was ready for the table. She filled a carafe of iced water, and they each carried part of the food.

After they sat down, Jo held out her hands to each side, palms up. Moirin and Heather each took one, then joined hands with Leslie.

"I know none of us are really religious, but I wanted to take a minute to be thankful," Jo said. "I heard something this morning that stuck with me, and I wanted to share it with you all. *Sweet friendships refresh the soul and awaken our hearts with joy. Never give up on a friend or abandon a friend of your father— for in the day of your brokenness you won't have to run to a relative for help. A friend nearby is better than a relative far away.* For me, that's all of you. I hope that you will always be my friends nearby."

Heather's chest constricted, and a lump formed in her throat. "Thank you. I feel the same way." She turned to Leslie. "You're my only blood relative, but you're also my friend. Thank you for being both." She reached over and stabbed two pancakes with her fork, then slid the platter closer to Leslie.

"Friends nearby," Moirin said. "I like that sentiment." She slid a few pieces of bacon onto her plate, then added a large spoonful of eggs, before passing the bowl to Jo.

Leslie sniffed, dabbing at the corner of her eye. "That was nice, Jo. Where did you hear it?" She piled three pancakes on her plate, then spooned the berry compote on top, licking her finger where the sweet syrup had dripped.

"I told Heather earlier that I went to church this morning. I do that sometimes." She shrugged at the mumbled surprise from Moirin. "I went to a cowboy church, and that was a Bible verse they read out of a modern translation. It resonated."

"I can't imagine not having you in my life. I don't have to see or talk to any of you every day, but you're there, like my favorite sneakers at the back of the closet. Ellis was more like that snuggly angora sweater I loved, but after too many washings, it got out of shape, and I finally had to let it go," Moirin said, tasting a forkful of eggs.

"Ha. That angora sweater. I remember. Oh, that first semester you were assigned as my roommate, you drove me crazy." Jo chuckled. "It was a gazillion years ago. I have to say, though, I liked you all from the first time we met."

"Eh," Heather said, setting her coffee cup down. "With me, it was touch and go, but you grew on me." She laughed at the outraged look on Jo's face. "Kidding. You are all my friends nearby."

"Well, I'm happy we've got each other. I thought about what you guys said, I realized you were right." She took a sip of coffee and proudly announced, "First thing this morning I called Kevin."

"Good for you." Moirin clapped softly. "How did it go?"

"So great, really. But then, Kevin's always a sweetheart. He agreed Mom and Dad should be comfortable financially, and it makes sense to review the budget before either of us just start putting money in their account. Maybe we need to do an insurance review, or get a new cell phone plan or something. We all know, there are lots of things that eat up the budget. He's going to arrange a night later this week. We'll go to our parents' house together and have an honest talk and look at everything."

"I'm so relieved," Jo said. "I was really worried you were so concerned with helping them that you would sacrifice your own safety net."

"That's the last thing I want to do," Jo admitted. "The past few years have been tough, but with that sale and the new job, I feel like the future is more secure. I need to protect that for myself, certainly, but also have a bit set aside in case they have an emergency down the line."

"That's smart. I hope it all goes well at your family meeting." Heather tried not to smile like an indulgent mother, but she was pleased they had been able to influence Jo to a reasonable compromise.

They finished breakfast, lingering at the table talking, and polishing off another pot of coffee, as the time edged toward mid-morning.

8
DEPARTURE

"Did you get the bags from your room?" Moirin heard Heather call out to Leslie from downstairs. She chuckled. *Always the mothering big sister.* Moirin turned back to her packing. A two-night trip shouldn't have required much, but between clothes, shoes, and a plethora of nighttime and morning moisturizers, special skincare routines, and makeup, it was an impressive pile. Once the bag was packed, she turned to the laptop and accessories, tucking them carefully into her briefcase. Once everything was neatly arranged, she checked the room again to ensure nothing was left behind.

The advice from Heather's great-grandmother came to her again. *Start as you mean to go on.* It crossed her mind several times since Heather had shared it, and this time, it spurred her to action. Glancing at her watch, she nodded, then picked up her phone and made a call.

"Moirin?"

"Good morning, Dad. I thought you might be getting back from brunch about now."

"Yes, honey, as always, you have impeccable timing."

"Wonderful," Moirin said. "I won't take much of your time."

"Sure. What's on your mind?"

"I'm thinking about the Board, and I was mulling over the suggestions in your email. I completely agree with your thoughts about

Gregorian Plankett. I've had a few unpleasant meetings with him and would not welcome him on our Board."

"As usual, we're of the same mind, then." She could hear her father's approval and satisfaction clearly, despite the warbly network connection.

"Partially." She took a deep breath. *Time to take a firm stance.* "In regard to the open seats for the Board, then, I understand your inclination to split the recommendation, taking one from me and one from Ian. I know in years passed, it's even been something you did alone or simply with Ian. I appreciate the acknowledgement of my position with the company now that you've included me in this decision."

"Yes, of course. You are the future of Garrett Diversified."

Moirin was empowered with that validation. "I'm glad you said that, Dad. It will only be a few years now until Uncle Ian retires, and I'll take over as CEO. I think that it will be best, both for the company now, as well as for my future transition, that all selections to the Board from this point forward be at my discretion, with you and the other board members approving."

"Not allow Ian input for the Board seats?" Charles took a heavy breath, and Moirin could hear him clucking his tongue thoughtfully. Had she been too hasty? It might have been better to ease into the idea and drop it like a bomb in his lap.

"It just makes sense. I don't want to be in a position of fighting for alternative energy solutions with a Board committed to oil and gas. Many of Ian's contemporaries do lean that way. I envision a future where we can be profitable without creating a negative impact on the environment. I'd like to pursue more of that now."

"Hm, you make a good point. At one point, Garrett was at the forefront of innovation, but I concede we're not leading in this area. We've only had a handful of your green projects approved, and you've proposed quite a few." Moirin could hear her father pacing, his wingtips clicking smartly on the wood floor of his home study. He always paced when assessing all sides of an issue. "You're right. Ian is the old guard, and you're the future. We're not quite the *Titanic*, but we can't turn on a dime. It takes planning. Now is the time to lay the foundation for the future."

"You'll back all my selections for the upcoming seats?"

"Yes. I'll take care of it with Ian. Make your choices and get them to me this week. I'll get them installed."

"Thank you, Dad. This is truly the best direction for the company. I appreciate your faith in me."

"You've proven yourself, Moirin. It doesn't take much faith when we all look at your track record. Drive safely back home. I'll stop by the office tomorrow."

"Perfect. Give Mother my love." She ended the call and sank onto the bed with a sigh of pure contentment. Sometimes, a problem hangs over you so heavily that its resolution brings a palpable sense of relief. This was one of those moments. She felt unburdened, almost buoyant with happiness.

Trying to hold back the grin, Moirin carried her bags down and stowed them in the truck. Jo must have brought hers down earlier because it was already tucked into the corner of the trunk. Coming back inside, she collected Orson's toys, water bowl, and food dish, storing them in the carrier under a blanket. She coaxed Orson in with kissing noises and a small treat.

"Time to go, buddy. A few house in the car, then I'll show you around your new home. It's a nice condo with a nice private courtyard. You're going to love it." I hope so. After his ordeal, he deserved a nice life. "I hope you're not too lonely when I'm working. Maybe you can help me with that, huh?"

A new chapter was unfolding. She would no longer face life alone. Orson could rely on her, and his presence was just what she needed. Both she and Ellis had embraced fresh beginnings; hers entirely on her own terms, without compromise. She had stood her ground for the board restructure, for once not accepting the docile and compliant role with the family patriarchs.

He strode regally, despite his limp, as if he were requesting transport and Moirin just the conveyance. She smiled, watching him, then carefully secured the latch and carried him into the house. Jo sat at the dining room table, and Moirin joined her there, setting Orson's carrier on the floor nearby. A faint me'ow of greeting emanated from inside.

"What can I do to help clean up?" Moirin asked.

Jo shifted her head, looking around the rooms. "I think it's all done. I have the leftover groceries bagged up in the refrigerator and started the dishwasher. Leslie and Heather are upstairs. She said the cleaning crew is coming tomorrow, so they'll take care of everything else."

Heather and Leslie tromped down the stairs, each dragging a suitcase. Moirin could hear as they dumped them near the front door, then came to the dining room.

Heather sank into a chair. "That was a workout." She dabbed at the sweat on her upper lip.

"I'm sad to go, guys. It's been so nice," Jo said.

"It has. But now that the world's gone back to normal, we can get together more often."

"I really enjoyed going out to dinner last night. I've missed our time together." Leslie pulled a chair out and sat down. "We should do this more often. Like, every Friday night. Just us girls."

"I like that idea, but Fridays are always so busy. How about a Tuesday? It's mid-week and usually a slow day," Moirin said.

"I love it. I'm in." Jo stuck her hand toward the center of the table, palm down. "I commit to meeting every Tuesday night for dinner as often as I can."

"Deal. Me too," Heather said, piling her hand on top of Jo's.

"I'll add it to my calendar." Moirin nodded, laying her hand on Heather's.

"Every Tuesday. Whoever can make it. No skipping it just because it's not all four of us," Leslie said, raising her right hand two fingers together, like an oath. She extended both hands, slapping one on top and the other on the bottom of the pile, sandwiching them together. "I love you guys."

"It's good we're all still here together. I feel like we're all entering this new phase of life. This time, it's not a matter of circumstances beyond our control. We can create whatever we want." Heather's face looked hopeful.

"What is it you want?" Moirin asked.

"I have no idea, but I guess that's what I get to figure out now," Heather said. "Make things nice for Tabor, taking care of Camilla when she lets me. How about you?" She looked at Jo.

"I'm going to be fabulous at my job, make sure everyone there loves me, and maybe invite the whole family over for Christmas this year."

"I'm going to inspire the minds of my students this year, keep trying to see my boys, and find some new hobbies, maybe. How about you, Moirin?"

"I think Orson and I are going to be very happy together." She folded her hands together and batted her eyes while the other three laughed.

Orson mewed pitifully from the carrier.

"I guess that's our cue to leave," Moirin said, standing up.

Moirin slid behind the wheel of the Audi as Jo climbed into the passenger seat. They clicked their seatbelts, and Moirin glanced in the back seat. Orson lay peacefully, his eyes barely open, purring. The carrier was secured by a complex web of seatbelts.

She chuckled. "Nice job on the restraints."

Jo grinned. "I improvised, but it works. We'll all get home safe."

The horn of the Pacifica blasted two short beeps. They glanced over. Heather lowered her window, and Jo did the same.

"Drive safe, guys. Dinner on Tuesday, right?"

"Absolutely. Safe travels," Moirin said as she leaned forward.

"Until Tuesday," Jo said.

"And the Tuesday after and the Tuesday after that," Leslie shouted as she waved wildly from beside Heather.

She backed down the driveway, feeling a sense of peace and warm friendship. Jo hummed under her breath as Orson's purring resonated from the back seat. Heather was right. It was a season of change, a new phase of life.

Big changes were coming, but not the ones they were expecting.

Author's Note
A Look at
Life's a Rodeo Series

Each book in this series focuses on a single character, exploring her personal and professional life challenges, struggles, accomplishments, and failures as she navigates midlife changes. Throughout her journey, she finds strength in herself and support from her friends.

The four main characters have their own distinct group dynamics and are not interchangeable, much like friendships in real life. In each book, one character often remains in the background, waiting to come forward in the next installment.

I've loved creating these characters and developing their stories to examine the real-life challenges of middle age, or second act, those *Thankful Intentionality* years, which come before the *Elder* years.

I hope you enjoy sharing this time in their lives and meeting the cowboys who provide them with new perspectives. The cowboy code and lifestyle depicted in these books reflect the philosophy rooted in the values of hard work, integrity, and self-reliance essential for surviving farm and ranch life in the American West.

Take a moment to explore the books that make up the series *Life's a Rodeo*....

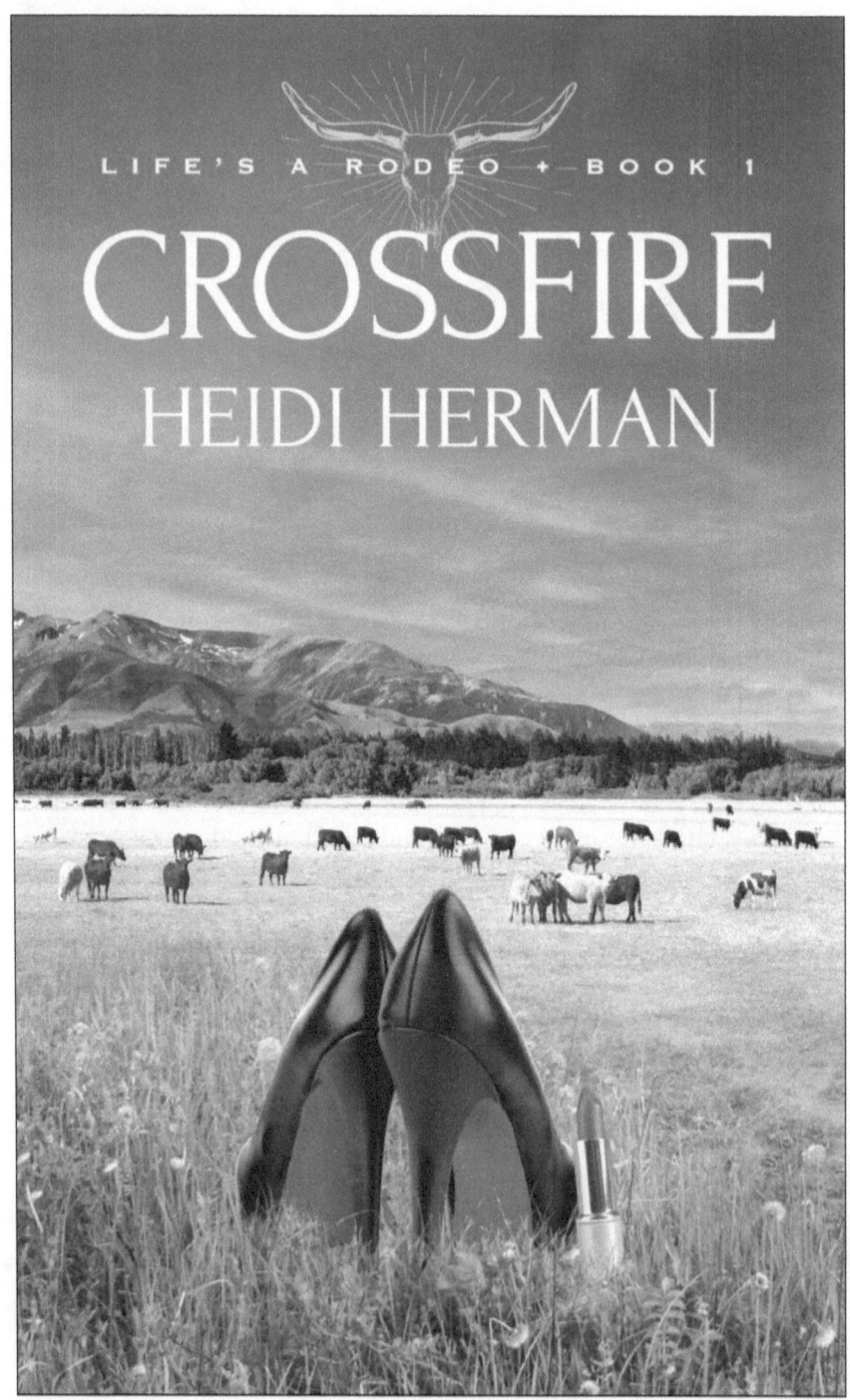

BOOK 1
CROSSFIRE
(MOIRIN'S STORY)

An aging, no-nonsense career energy executive reconsiders her life after she becomes involved with a cowboy while working to save her professional reputation and protect the future of her family's business.

Everyone around her marked the passage of time through celebrations of weddings, anniversaries, and graduations, measuring life success through joy in family portraits. Everyone else had a life with husbands and wives, children, and grandchildren. Moirin Garrett has a cat named Orson.

After decades spent building her grandfather's Denver-based energy company into an international corporation, she's poised to be the next CEO, achieving the pinnacle of business success. When the Board of Directors announced a rigorous vetting process, ostensibly to avoid nepotism, it should have been a formality. But the challenges of an environmental impact study, a vindictive business associate, and a string of increasingly suspicious management issues that leave her leadership skills in question may put her professional future and personal legacy in jeopardy.

When she meets a state brand inspector and a team roping cowboy named Jace, his pragmatic outlook and life philosophy challenge her ideas about the environment, life, and the concept of legacy. On the verge of achieving everything she'd worked for, Moirin Garrett wonders—had she made the right choices in life? At this stage, was it too late to change her path?

BOOK 2
FULL GO ROUND
(JO'S STORY)

When a single morning's ritual turns sour—thanks to a smoking toaster, a failing water heater, and a stormy reminder of life's unpredictability—Jo never suspects that the real upheaval lies ahead.

It wasn't the life she had planned, but Josephine Sandersen was content enough. Childless and widowed early in life, her home was her one secure place.

When a sudden storm threatens an already dilapidated roof, she scrambles to pay a contractor whose inspection list keeps adding to her necessary house repairs. A tight budget and dwindling nest egg has her stretching to meet the obligations. But when her marketing career unravels, the situation becomes dire. Jo is desperate to find work before she loses her home.

An apathetic headhunter, ageist hiring managers, and constant family demands make the job hunt seem impossible. When her best friend invites her to a team roping competition, a chance opportunity draws her into the world of rodeo announcing. What started as a part-time job to pay the bills turns into a life-changing experience, and a spark of something more with her new boss, a cowboy named Reece, who seems determined to irritate her into shedding her people-pleasing ways.

Torn between the desire for family acceptance and the chance to be independent and chase her dreams, Jo must decide: is it too late to claim the life—and the love—she never dared imagine?

COMING 2026: BOOK 3
ROUGHSTOCK
(HEATHER'S STORY)

Heather Santos has always been the dependable one—an accomplished Denver physical therapist, devoted mother to a newly minted med student, and wife to a celebrated physician. When her clinic assigns her to develop a daring fitness-and-intimacy workshop for the over-50 crowd, Heather thinks things can't get worse—but nothing prepares her for the real shock. In the span of weeks, her husband asks for a divorce, her daughter relocates to California, and the spacious home she once took pride in becomes a haunting reminder that life rarely follows a neat script.

Thrown into uncharted territory, Heather sets out to rediscover herself. She stumbles through cooking classes, fumbles on the pickleball court, and stalks online dating profiles, one in particular catching her eye, but she's unable to make a move. In an unlikely encounter at a rodeo arena, she's shocked to come face-to-face with the object of her fascination—a no-nonsense cowboy and large animal veterinarian named Elias. Helping her conquer her many fears, Elias and a special Icelandic horse teach her that courage isn't the absence of fear but the art of moving forward anyway. As Heather struggles to overcome her phobias, she must also confront her own ingrained patterns: Can a woman who's spent decades caring for everyone else learn to design a life that thrills her, even at fifty-plus?

Equal parts laugh-out-loud comedy and tender self-revelation, this is a story of midlife reinvention, surprising romance, and the hard-won wisdom that true comfort comes when you dare to leave your old habits behind. Join Heather on her unexpected journey—and discover how a broken heart can become the kick-start to a braver, brighter future.

COMING 2026: BOOK 4
RERIDE
(LESLIE'S STORY)

At fifty-two, Leslie James, an elementary school teacher, is used to teaching people how to get up. She's overcome a prescription drug addiction and kept sober for five years, and though she's worked to fix her relationships, she remains estranged from her teenage sons. Her sunny disposition masks the fear of being alone, facing the ravages of menopause, and growing old. She's obsessed with hobbies from fitness to photography, desperate to stay busy and useful.

When she joins a dating app to help her newly divorced older sister, Heather, overcome dating fears, Leslie expects an awkward small talk and left-swipe situation. What she doesn't expect is a message from Riley, a twelve-year-old "matchmaker" determined to find a girlfriend for her own rodeo-dad. Riley's mother, battling her own demons, checked into rehab and vanished, leaving the girl in limbo until Riley tracked Wes down on her own.

Leslie's own mother died of an overdose, and this shared loss draws them together. When they discover a surprising passion for old Norse legends, Leslie and Riley form a secret friendship. But when Wes comes home early and finds Leslie in his living room, confusion escalates to anger. Riley bolts, and Wes stumbles in pursuit, aggravating an old knee injury. With no health insurance and in the height of rodeo season, Wes risks losing both his livelihood and his newly discovered daughter. Leslie coerces Heather, a physical therapist, to aid Wes.

Determined to help Wes keep his job, ensuring he and Riley have a chance at becoming a family, Leslie steps into the world of rodeos, cowboys, and untamed horses. As she helps him reclaim his strength, she learns to trust that she is worthy of a second chance. And when the dust settles, what began as a cautious friendship might just bloom into a new family.

ABOUT THE AUTHOR

 Heidi Herman is an author of books in several genres, but has a special love for women's fiction. She favors writing stories of strong women who face and overcome obstacles to live their best lives. Her passion and a common theme in her writing is her Icelandic heritage.

She started her writing journey with children's books and folklore, and in addition to fiction, has written a motivational book for adults and two cookbooks. In addition to writing, she loves cooking, photography, travel, and exploring the outdoors. She spends her time writing, researching Iceland, attending Scandinavian events, and pursuing adventure all along the way.

Website: www.heidihermanauthor.com

Instagram: https://www.instagram.com/heidihermanauthor

Facebook: https://www.facebook.com/HeidiHermanAuthor

If you enjoyed this book, please consider sharing your comments in a review on Goodreads or your favorite retailer. Reviews from readers like you are so important to the success of independent writers like me, and I sincerely appreciate the feedback.

Other Books by Heidi Herman

FICTION
Crossfire
Her Viking Heart

NON-FICTION
The Hidden Vegetables Cookbook:
90 Tasty Recipes for Veggie-Averse Adults

On With the Butter!
Spread More Living onto Everyday Life
Homestyle Icelandic Cooking for American Kitchens
(with Íeda Jónasdóttir Herman)

SHORT STORY COLLECTION
The Guardians of Iceland and Other Icelandic Folk Tales

CHILDREN'S BOOKS
Yule Lads Legend: Iceland's Jólasveinar

The Icelandic Yule Lads: Mayhem at the North Pole

www.ingramcontent.com/pod-product-compliance
Lightning Source LLC
LaVergne TN
LVHW090036080526
838202LV00046B/3834